UNCONDITIONAL SURRENDER

"Frank," Rachel Marron said quietly, "I want you to know that nothing that's happened between us matters."

Her voice cracked and her shoulders drooped and she seemed to wilt for a moment. Then she composed herself, squaring her shoulders. "I need you . . . I'm afraid . . . and I hate it. I hate my fear. Please protect me."

"I can't protect you here," said Frank. "It's impossible. The odds are on his side. I want to take you away for a while."

"But I have the Oscars coming up on the—"

Frank shot her a look.

"I'm sorry, I'm sorry," she said. "Where are we going?"

"Somewhere people don't know about," Frank said. "And if you cross me this time, I'll kill you myself."

THE BODYGUARD

ROBERT TINE

THE BODYGUARD

A NOVEL BASED ON THE SCREENPLAY BY LAWRENCE KASDAN

A SIGNET BOOK

SIGNET
Published by the Penguin Group
Penguin Books USA Inc., 375 Hudson Street,
New York, New York 10014, U.S.A.
Penguin Books Ltd, 27 Wrights Lane, London W8 5TZ, England
Penguin Books Australia Ltd, Ringwood, Victoria, Australia
Penguin Books Canada Ltd, 10 Alcorn Avenue,
Toronto, Ontario, Canada M4V 3B2
Penguin Books (N.Z.) Ltd, 182-190 Wairau Road, Auckland 10, New Zealand

Penguin Books Ltd, Registered Offices: Harmondsworth, Middlesex, England

Published by Signet, an imprint of New American Library,
a division of Penguin Books USA Inc.

First Printing, December, 1992
10 9 8 7 6 5 4 3 2 1

There were three shots from two guns. First one shot, then, quickly, two more answered. The muzzle flashes seemed to punch bright white holes in the darkness. Then there came the sound of bodies falling to the concrete.

There was enough light in the parking garage for Frank Farmer to see his target, a heavy-set man in a dark suit, slump against the body of a long Cadillac stretch limousine and then slowly slip to the floor, his track greased by the great gout of blood streaming from his back.

There was a large, red, ragged hole where the man's heart had once beat. Farmer stared at the wound, puzzled. It seemed to have been wrapped in dark green paper, tatters stuck to the fabric and gore. Then he realized. The two bullets he had fired into the man's body must have driven through a wallet strategically placed over the hit man's heart, driving scraps of money into the wound. Farmer nodded to himself – that was what this whole case had been about: money.

'Jesus Christ, Farmer!'

Frank Farmer was lying across the thin back of Stanley Klingman, pressing the nattily dressed financier into the hard dirty floor, the lapel of his Armani suit soaking up a pool of oil as thick as congealed blood. A split second before the first shot Farmer had thrown himself against Klingman, knocking him to the floor and landing on him heavily, like a wrestler pinning his opponent, shielding his client with his own

I

body. A bullet had smashed into the window of Klingman's Bentley, but before the glass fell to the cement floor Farmer had fired his two deadly shots.

Klingman tried to push off the weight of Farmer's body, but he was shoved back down. The bodyguard swept the acre of concrete with his gun, listening to footsteps running toward him.

A man rounded the limo, his eyes growing wide at the sight of the body and the blood. He wore a peaked cap. The limousine was his, a chauffeur.

'Freeze,' ordered Farmer.

The chauffeur looked at the gun in Frank Farmer's hand and did as he was told. He froze and raised his hands, as if he was the victim of a hold up.

Frank Farmer's voice was calm, but he was issuing an order, there was no mistaking that. 'Call the police.'

The chauffeur nodded and ran.

Farmer relaxed and got to his feet. Klingman exhaled heavily and stood. His handsome face was bleached white and he trembled as if cold.

'Jesus Christ . . .' he sighed and wiped his brow.

It took thirteen hours for Frank Farmer to deal with the homicide cops and the crime scene cops and the evidence cops and the forensics guys and the background investigation cops, the Feds, the Narcs and the New York State Task Force guys, the RICO cops, the DA's investigator and some pain in the neck from the Securities and Exchange Commission who was bound to show up at any crime scene that involved a high flying arbitrageur like Klingman.

Thirteen hours was an express job for the New York City Police Department and its many pilot fish because before Farmer had turned private he had worked for Treasury, known to the public as the Secret Service.

Frank had been one of them, an insider in law enforcement and there was a certain professional courtesy that cops extended to other cops, even alumni.

Frank rushed through the system in thirteen hours, culminating in the District Attorney empaneling a Grand Jury to determine if laws had been broken – and if Frank Farmer had broken them – in the killing of Franco 'Fat Frank' Manganaro. Grand Juries always did exactly what prosecutors told them to do – they would indict a ham sandwich, as the old joke went – and the prosecutor on the case suggested that Mr Farmer had been licensed to carry a concealed weapon and to use it in his defense and that Mr Manganaro, a freelance thug from Philadelphia, had richly deserved his abrupt demise. The Grand Jury did not indict and Frank Farmer was given his gun and told he was free to go.

He went directly to his hotel and packed his suitcase, then he caught a cab up to Klingman's majestic apartment building on Fifth Avenue facing the Metropolitan Museum of Art.

During the thirteen hours Frank Farmer had been seeing that justice was done, Klingman had retreated to his apartment, slept a while and then had put himself in the hands of his masseuse, barber, manicurist and valet. He looked fresh and well groomed, but just beneath the surface he could still feel the fear and the jitters. Frank, in his crumpled suit, looked exhausted but calm.

Notwithstanding the searing moment of violence and the bureaucratic wrangle that followed, the Klingman case had not been a particularly difficult one. Farmer's client had made the mistake of testifying against some of his brother Wall Streeters, his testimony sending two men to jail. One of them swore

3

revenge and the encounter with 'Fat Frank' Manganaro had been the result. For a month Frank Farmer had shadowed Klingman waiting for the attack. When it came, he dealt with it. End of story.

Klingman led Farmer into the wood-paneled study and poured two snifters of brandy. He handed one to Farmer.

'Your hands ever shake, Frank?'

Farmer smiled slightly. 'Sometimes. It's nothing. Nothing more than a shot of adrenalin.'

Klingman nodded to himself. 'Mind if I ask you a question?'

Farmer shook his head. 'What's on your mind?'

'How did you know?'

'Know?'

'About Manganaro. How did you know he was going to try something?'

'I didn't know it would be him. I hadn't even heard of him until it was all over. He's just a goon for hire.' He shrugged. 'You were threatened. I knew someone would try something. Eventually.'

'But when . . . when it happened, you *knew* that it was happening, it was like you looked a few seconds into the future and saw it happen before it did.'

Frank Farmer allowed himself a little smile. 'He gave himself away. I saw him.'

'Hell,' Klingman said, laughing. '*I* saw him too. It didn't mean a thing to me. He was just some guy in a parking garage.'

'He was washing his car,' said Farmer, as if that explained everything.

'So?'

'They don't wash cars on the parking levels. He gave himself away.'

Klingman shook his head, as if in wonder. 'I guess I

was lucky to have gotten you on my side.' He slipped an envelope out of the inside breast pocket of his suit jacket and handed it to Frank. He didn't open it, hardly looked at it, and slid it into his own pocket.

'Thank you,' he said.

'You know,' said Klingman, 'I'd like you to stay on. Make this a permanent position. You could name your price.'

Farmer shook his head. 'I'm not good in permanent positions. My feet go to sleep.' Klingman could tell by the tone of the bodyguard's voice that he would never change his mind. Money would not alter that fact.

He raised his glass as if in salute. 'Thank you for saving my life,' he said. Klingman drank deep, as if he needed the alcohol to steady his nerves. Farmer did not even raise the glass to his lips.

CHAPTER ONE

The objects were arranged on the surface of the battered old desk with military precision. There was a stack of white typing paper, a jar of glue, a pair of scissors, a stack of magazines, a box of tight-fitting latex surgical gloves and a TV remote control. The television was on, tuned to MTV. The volume was turned down low but the music accompanying the flashy images was audible. It was Rachel Marron singing her colossal hit 'I Have Nothing'.

He reached into the box of gloves and put them on, snapping the bands tight around his wrists. Carefully, he picked up the magazine on the top of the stack. It was *Screen Stars*, a tacky tabloid filled with adoring articles chronicling the doings of the reigning names of Hollywood. The cover was a riot of photographs and noisy headlines but the lead story screamed: 'RACHEL MARRON'S GREATEST TRIUMPH!'

He examined the headline for a moment, then, with the meticulous care of a surgeon he picked up the scissors and carefully cut the words 'Rachel Marron' from the magazine cover. Then he cut the name in half, excising the 'Rachel'.

Painstakingly, he applied glue to the back of the slip of paper and laid it down on a clean sheet of typing paper. Working methodically through his stack of magazines, he slowly assembled a note. Although he cut his words and letters from different magazines and typefaces, he worked with such care in building his message, that the note had an unusually neat appearance and was quite easy to read.

His neat, almost fussy handiwork belied the repellent words he had so patiently assembled. When he had finished, the note read: 'MARRON BITCH – YOU HAVE EVERYTHING. I HAVE NOTHING. THE TIME TO DIE IS COMING.'

A crowd can turn into a mob in a matter of seconds, all that is required is a spark. The huge throng that had assembled at the Long Beach Coliseum for a sold-out Rachel Marron concert was edging toward the brink, pushing toward turning from a crowd of adoring fans into a delirious, out of control swarm.

The spark was Rachel Marron. When her dove-gray Cadillac limousine pulled up in front of the theater, the fans milling at the entrance rushed toward the car, pressing against the doors, trapping the object of their love inside the vehicle.

The theater security guards managed to get them back from the car and hustled Rachel through the crowd. Hands reached out to snatch at her, touch her clothing, her hair, as if she was some kind of good luck talisman, as if some of her stardom would rub off her and enrich their own lives.

They chanted: 'Rachel! Rachel! Rachel!'

Rachel Marron's smile was fixed on her face, but she had her head down and her shoulder turned protectively against her fans as the security guards plowed a path through the crowd like icebreakers.

In Rachel's wake came her entourage, the friends and family, the managers and handlers, the hangers-on that always seem to surround celebrities. From the crowd came gifts, offerings for the star from her loyal fans. The entourage gathered them. Flowers, greeting cards, notes, tapes, autograph books and then, out of the thicket of hands, a little doll wrapped in a ribbon sash: 'Rachel We Love You!' carefully lettered across the chest. An urgent hand pressed it on Rachel's make-up girl and she took it.

Then she was gone. The doors of the Coliseum closed behind her and the crowd seemed to sag, disappointed and exhausted, worn out by the few minutes of frenzy.

Inside the building, Rachel Marron shook her head. 'Whew, I'm glad that's over.'

Nicki, Rachel's sister and confidante, patted her lightly on the shoulder. 'They just love you, that's all.'

'They sure have a funny way of showing it.'

An assistant stage manager was waiting for her. 'Rachel,' he said urgently, 'make-up is waiting.'

Thirty-five minutes later, Rachel strode on to the great wide stage and felt the applause and cheers, the noise from the audience buffeting her like waves on a windswept beach. It was an electrifying moment, an instant of pure unadulterated adoration that pumped energy and power into her like a drug. It was what she lived for.

The excitement carried backstage, pulsing in the dressing room, thrilling Rachel Marron's entourage. They couldn't be her, but they were close to her, absorbing some of her reflected glory. There was chatter and laughter, and a stirring sense that they were part of something great, something unique.

Scattered around the room were the gifts and the bunches of flowers, forgotten now that the show was about to begin. All eyes were focused on the television monitors showing the action on stage.

'She is *on*!' shouted someone.

'Go get 'em, Rachel!'

9

'Give 'em hell!'

And she did. A delighted roar went up from the crowd when the first notes of 'I Have Nothing' came up from the band, but in that instant the applause, the music and Rachel's voice were obscured when the little doll sitting next to one of the monitors exploded.

There was a sudden flash of flame and then the dressing room filled with smoke and screams. The TV shattered, glass showering. The room filled with an acrid, electric smell and the lights burnt out.

The entourage panicked. People fell to the floor and shouted, everyone sure that they were dead, that their lives were over.

On stage, blissfully unaware, her audience enrapt, Rachel Marron sang on. As the honied lyrics of her hit song flowed out into the darkened auditorium, she sang as if her life depended on it, as if she had to transmit her love for her fans, not knowing that one of them was trying to kill her.

CHAPTER TWO

All was calm and quiet in the scruffy back yard of Frank Farmer's small suburban home. It was just the way he liked things.

Constant vigilance was wearing, continual suspicion was corrosive, a strain that ground him down as if he had been applied to a whetstone. But Frank Farmer had a tried and true, if not particularly unusual antidote to the stresses of his peculiar profession. It was his habit to take a long vacation after each job, a series of long lazy days during which he did little besides read and sleep, recharging his batteries and decompressing like a diver coming up from the depths.

He lazed on a battered chaise-longue, wearing a pair of old shorts, sun glasses slipping down his nose. Next to him on a squat metal table was a glass of ice tea sweating in the sun and a decidedly low-tech old transistor radio. It was tuned to an oldies station, 'Don't Walk Away Renée' playing quietly.

A lawn sprinkler waved back and forth, scattering water like soft rain on the scraggly grass. Frank didn't really care about his lawn. He liked the soothing sound.

Stretched out in his back yard, soaking up the sun, Frank Farmer didn't look like the bodyguard. A stranger passing by would have thought that Frank was probably not all that different from his neighbors – middle-class, middle-management, middle-of-the-road, middle-America.

The only clue that suggested that Frank Farmer was

different, that he wasn't just another working stiff in a nondescript neighborhood, were the eight double-edged throwing knives that were scattered on the grass next to him, glinting in the sun.

He wasn't asleep, he wasn't even dozing, he was just on stand down, at rest but still aware. As Farmer relaxed, his mind kept track of sounds and sensations. He heard the low mutter of a lawn mower a couple of houses over, the sizzle and smell of hamburgers on a grill next door. A dog barking across the street. A few blocks away the brief howl as a car alarm started and was hastily turned off. Everything was normal.

Then Frank Farmer heard a car pull up in front of his house. It was not a suburban station wagon or down at the heels hatchback. The engine note was low and throaty, a powerful sports car, unusual in that neighborhood.

The car came to a halt and the engine died. A car door slammed and then, a few seconds later, the doorbell inside his house chimed.

Farmer raised himself on one elbow and shouted: 'Out back.'

A tall man came around the side of the house. Behind his shades, Farmer examined him closely. He was fiftyish and distinguished-looking, a light-skinned black man dressed casually but expensively. No jewelry. His lightweight silk sports coat was cut a little too tight for him to be carrying a gun. He was not a threat.

'Mr Farmer?'

Frank started to swing up out of the chaise-longue. 'Um-hm.'

'Please, don't get up.' The man pushed the air in front of him, as if gently nudging Farmer back down.

'Okay.' He shrugged and lay back.

'Bill Devaney,' said the man, his hand out. They shook hands. 'It's a pleasure to meet you.'

Farmer smiled. 'What can I do for you, Mr Devaney?'

'Bill.'

'Bill.' Frank Farmer raised an eyebrow quizzically.

'Frank,' said Devaney, 'what you can do for me is solve a very big problem. That's what you can do for me.'

'And what problem would that be?'

'I would like to hire you to protect someone. Someone important. Someone famous.'

'Show business?'

Bill Devaney smiled. He took this as a good sign. Everyone loved show business, everyone in his world counted it a privilege to be around celebrities. This Frank Farmer, it seemed, was no different from anybody else.

'That's right. A very big name. The biggest.'

Farmer shook his head. 'I'm sorry, Mr Devaney –'

'Bill.'

'I'm sorry, Bill. I'm not in the business of protecting celebrities. I hope this hasn't been too much of a waste of time for you.' Frank Farmer's voice definitely suggested that their meeting and acquaintance was at an end.

Devaney's face fell. 'But . . . don't you even want to know who it is?'

'Nope.'

'It's Rachel Marron,' said Devaney as if he hadn't heard Frank's negative reply. 'I'm her personal manager. I take care of her.' Then, realizing what he had said, he added: 'Up to a point I take care of her. There are some things that require more specialized skills. That's where you come in.'

If Farmer was a big fan of Rachel Marron he didn't show it. In fact, he gave no indication that he even recognized the name. He shrugged, noncommittal.

'Rachel Marron,' Devaney repeated. 'The hottest name in show business and you won't protect her.'

'That's right.'

'*Because* she's in show business.'

'I told you, I don't do celebrities.'

'But the biggest money is in show business,' protested Bill Devaney.

Frank Farmer shrugged again and closed his eyes behind his sun glasses.

Devaney stared at him a moment. It was his experience that money, particularly large sums of it, turned most heads. Up until now he had found that he could always buy his way in the entertainment world. Farmer's lack of interest in money exasperated him – and it intrigued him too. He decided to change tactics.

Devaney bent and picked up one of the throwing knives. Set in the ground about fifteen feet from where he stood was a stout wooden post. It was pockmarked with slim knife holes and gouges where blades had hit but gone wide.

Holding the knife by the blade, Devaney threw the weapon, launching toward the stake. It missed by three feet and clattered against the fence that divided Farmer's property from his neighbor's. The sound made Farmer open his eyes for a moment to see what was going on. He looked, then closed them again.

'Do you really do these things? The knives, I mean,' Devaney asked.

Frank Farmer did not bother to answer. It seemed self-evident that eight knives, plus a post to throw them at would suggest that, yes indeed, he did have an interest in throwing knives.

'Isn't she the one who collects dolls?' asked Frank Farmer. He was largely immune to popular culture. He rarely went to current, first run movies, never read a gossip column, his consumption of television, restricted mostly to Cable News Network, was way below the national average. But one couldn't be alive in the United States without some knowledge of celebrity seeping into consciousness. Something – an article in an airline magazine, newspaper headline glimpsed out of the corner of his eye, a snatch of overheard conversation – made him connect Rachel Marron with a collection of dolls.

Bill Devaney was exasperated. 'Farmer, Rachel Marron is one of the most famous people in America. She's won every music award invented. She's got the number one song in the country right now. "I Have Nothing". You know it?'

'I don't think so,' said Farmer. He didn't open his eyes. 'Maybe if you sang a couple of verses . . .'

Devaney couldn't tell if Farmer was serious or if he was pulling his leg. He was used to being in control, but he wasn't here and he didn't like it. 'C'mon, *Rachel Marron* – the star of the movie *Queen of the Night*? Her first picture and she'll probably be nominated for an Oscar. Stars don't come any bigger and you want to know if she's the one who collects dolls?'

Frank Farmer opened his eyes and looked at Devaney over the top of his sun glasses. 'You mean, she *isn't* the one who collects dolls?'

Bill Devaney shrugged, defeated. 'Yes. She's the one who collects dolls.'

Frank nodded, as if confirming something to himself. He lay back on the chaise. 'I thought I knew who she was.'

Devaney picked up another one of the knives,

turning it over in his hands, staring at the polished blade. 'You're probably deadly with these things, aren't you?'

'Deadly,' deadpanned Frank.

'Show me.'

Frank did not move.

Devaney shook his head. 'Why are you resisting this job?' he demanded. 'It's a big one . . .' He stared at Frank's impassive face. 'Two thousand bucks a week.'

The figure was as effective as the knife Devaney had thrown a few moments earlier. 'Okay . . . okay. Twenty-five hundred a week.'

'There are several good men available for that kind of money.' Frank Farmer still had not opened his eyes, but at least Devaney had provoked him into responding. It was better than nothing.

'Yeah, but –'

'Have you talked to Fitzgerald or Racine? Portman? They're all good. Very good.'

'Yeah,' said Bill Devaney, 'Portman was interested, but –'

'Then get Portman.'

Devaney sensed an opening. Maybe Farmer could be talked around now that the names of his rivals had come up. It was time for a little stroking.

'Portman was interested, but we were told that you were the best. Not Portman.'

'The best? There's no such thing as the best.'

It was cards-on-the-table time. 'Farmer, never mind that she's a celebrity, never mind the show business – we are talking about a very frightened lady. A very frightened lady who has a seven-year-old son. Believe me, I wouldn't be here if I didn't think this was for real.' The urgency in his voice grew a little more intense. 'Farmer,' he said, 'she *begged* me to get you.

Look, pack a bag, come up to the house, stay a few days. Take a look. What can that hurt?'

Frank took in this information, then he sat up and took off his sun glasses and stared at Devaney for a long moment. He picked up five of the throwing knives, holding them between the knuckles of his right hand.

'All right. I'll come and I'll look the situation over. If I take the job, it's three thousand a week.'

Devaney whistled hoarsely, quietly. 'Three thousand a week? You must be very deadly for that kind of money. Okay. Three thousand it is.'

As if to establish his credentials as a deadly sort of guy, Frank turned to face the post, squaring his shoulders and raising one of the knives. He threw it hard and wild, the knife wobbling through the air raggedly. It missed the post by a good six feet and it clattered against the fence, just as Devaney's lame attempt had done. In fact, Devaney's knife had been markedly closer to the post than Farmer's.

'Shit,' said Frank.

Devaney's face fell.

Frank Farmer examined the next blade as if instructions for proper use were inscribed on the blade.

'I know it's something like . . .' Frank mumbled, twisting his wrist a couple of times, as if practising throws. He brought his arm back and tossed the next one, the knife getting away from him at the top of his arc. The blade whistled by Devaney and vanished into a clump of bushes.

'Hey, Farmer, for God's sake!' Devaney scrambled out of the way, positioning himself in the safest place he could see – right behind Frank.

'Sorry about that,' said Farmer with a weak smile. He raised his hand to throw the next knife, then

17

paused. 'You know, you shouldn't stand right behind me like that . . . These things can get away from you and I wouldn't want you to get hurt.'

Devaney scurried to one side. Farmer fired the next knife. It spun through the air, turning tight, flashing silver cartwheels, end over end, straight and true. The point sunk two inches into the post. A split second later the next knife thudded into the wood, then the third.

Devaney blinked. There was a perfect straight line of knives in the post. Then he smiled. 'Deadly.'

Farmer shrugged. 'Deadly enough.'

CHAPTER THREE

You are what you drive, at least that's what they say in Los Angeles. If that was the case, then Frank Farmer's dusty, dun-colored Chevrolet Caprice Classic marked him as clearly as if he wore a sign around his neck. The down-at-the-heel automobile proclaimed: 'I am nobody. Pay no attention to me.' And that was fine with Frank – except when he was driving in LA's toniest neighborhoods. In amongst the Ferrari Testarossas and the Bentley Mulsannes and the other half-million dollar cars so common in Bel Air and Beverly Hills, Frank's Chevy stood out. It said: 'I don't belong here.'

He pulled his car to a halt in front of Rachel Marron's home a few minutes early for his appointment. Killing the engine, he got out of the car and surveyed the house and the quiet street.

The Marron estate was on Waverly Lane in Bel Air, a two-and-a-half-acre chunk of very expensive real estate. The house was a rambling *mélange* of architectural styles set in the middle of a series of lush lawns and formal gardens with a series of terraces descending toward the street. Scattered around the grounds were the standard movie-star requirements – a large, sparkling blue swimming pool and a couple of clay-surfaced tennis courts.

Peering through the big wrought-iron gates up the curving drive, one could see only a small part of the house, the rest of the building obscured by arbor and shrubbery. The whole compound was surrounded by a tall stone wall that could have been climbed by anyone with all their limbs intact.

Frank Farmer nodded when he saw it – things were just as he expected them to be. It was the usual Hollywood fortress-as-home reasoning: if they, the 'they' every star feared yet needed – the fans, the tourists, the kooks and crazies – couldn't see you, then you were safe. Of course, the inverse was true: if you couldn't see them, you didn't know if they were there.

Frank Farmer took in all of this with a hard stare that lasted only a few seconds. Where other people saw a luxurious and impregnable mansion he saw an expensive security risk, which, far from being invulnerable, was almost tragically easy to invade. But he didn't see things the way other people saw them. His living, his life and the lives of the people he was hired to protect required that he live in a state of heightened vigilance and heightened awareness. Nothing was trivial, beneath notice. He could never ignore the mundane details of daily living because he could never be sure when something might emerge suddenly and with lethal significance.

There was an intercom speaker set in the concrete-and-stucco gate post, but Frank didn't go to it immediately. Instead, he grabbed one of the wrought-iron cross-beams of the tall gates and threw his weight back, rocking the gates on their rusty hinges. You wouldn't need anything heavier than a pick-up truck to smash through and be up the driveway before anyone in the house was any the wiser. Devaney had been right. Rachel Marron and her son needed protection – from her own security, if nothing else.

Backing away from the gates, Frank Farmer had a sudden and clear sense of being watched. Not from the house or from any concealed surveillance device, but from behind, as there was a curious prickling sensation on the back of his neck.

He turned. Parked a few hundred yards down Waverly Lane was a black Toyota, a 4 × 4 rough-terrain vehicle, riding high on its suspension. It was too far off to read the license plate or to make out the driver, and in the same instant that Frank took a step toward it the big engine burst into life and the car took off down the street. It moved quickly – not recklessly, but fast enough to be suspicious. He made the first of many mental notes, to check out black Toyota 4 × 4s. It would be futile – there must be thousands of them in LA – but it was not something he could afford to ignore.

Frank slipped behind the wheel of his car, pulled it up until he was level with the intercom voice box recessed in the wall and rang the call button. He waited a moment, then, with a blizzard of static, came a man's voice. The transmission was terrible.

'Yes?'

'Frank Farmer to see Miss Marron.'

'Huh? What?'

Frank shook his head in disgust. 'Alexander Graham Bell to see Miss Marron.'

Either the man on the other end of the line had not heard or he thought that the inventor of the telephone had come to call.

'Have you got an appointment?'

'The atomic number of zinc is thirty,' said Frank.

'All right.'

There was a loud buzzing and the electric lock unclasped and the gates began to swing open, slowly and jittery, as if the metal was infused with arthritis.

Frank drove through and watched the gates in his rear-view mirror. The gates stood open long enough to drive not one vehicle through but three or four. More bad news. He scanned the grounds, running his professional eye over the terrain. There were lots of pretty gardens and shady spots, trees with low-hanging branches. It was not a lush and luxuriant garden to Farmer – it was just a collection of good hiding places.

There was a circular turn-around in front of the porte-cochère of the Marron house, but Frank did not park there. He pulled into the garage area, coming to a halt next to a pink Jaguar XKE. A chauffeur was polishing the leaping jaguar on the hood with his left hand. His right hand was heavily bandaged. He was a slim, tall black man. Frank judged him to be somewhere in his middle twenties.

When Frank's car rolled to a halt, the chauffeur put down his cloth and peered suspiciously at Farmer. A painter's truck was pulled up next to the garage and two men were unloading equipment.

Farmer wondered what kind of security check they had been subjected to.

'Can I help you?' asked the chauffeur.

'Are you the man on the intercom?'

The chauffeur shook his head. 'No. Can I help you?'

'My name is Edison. I have an appointment today with Miss Marron.'

'Oh?' The driver was still suspicious and Frank liked that. It was the first and only sign of security he had encountered. He hoped that most of the staff were at least as vigilant. 'And that was arranged by . . .?'

'Mr Devaney arranged it.'

The chauffeur's misgivings vanished. He gestured toward the wide white front door like a headwaiter. 'Then go right ahead, Mr Edison.'

Frank Farmer frowned. The chauffeur just lost all

his hard-won points. He started toward the door, then stopped and turned back to face the young man. 'What happened to your arm?'

The chauffeur grimaced and looked at his bandage. 'A doll,' he said, sourly. He returned to the Jaguar and started polishing again.

Frank rang the doorbell and waited. The door was unlocked, slightly ajar.

After a moment, the door swung open. The house-keeper was a warm, matronly woman in her fifties. She smiled pleasantly.

'Henry Ford to see Mr Devaney,' said Frank.

'Come in please, Mr Ford. I'm Emma.'

'How do you do?' Frank was standing in a wide entrance hall, the dark-blue tiled floor buffed to a high gloss. There was a heavy, carved credenza against one wall, a large vase of flowers placed in the center of the dark marble top. A gracefully curved staircase swept up to the upper floors.

Emma did not stand on ceremony. 'I'll tell you quite honestly, Mr Ford, I don't know where Mr Devaney is. Did he say he would be here?'

Frank nodded. 'Yes, he did.'

Emma shrugged and smiled, beaming as if she and Frank were sharing a private joke. 'Well, if he said it, he probably is. Let me look around.'

She led Frank into a large, obviously rarely used formal parlor. Painters were working in the room and they had covered the furniture with dustsheets to pro-tect the pieces from the paint, but Farmer could tell that they were substantial and antique. The drop cloths didn't quite reach the floor and peeping out here and there were the ball-and-claw feet of old chairs and sofas.

The dominant feature of the room was a huge

television set on which Rachel Marron's 'I Have Nothing' video was playing. The song could be heard through speakers concealed somewhere in the room.

'Please make yourself at home,' said Emma. 'Can I get you anything?'

'No, thank you.'

'I'll be back in a moment.' Emma left him standing in the middle of the room, heading back the way they came, toward the foyer. Frank watched her go, then walked away, moving off through the house, going in the opposite direction.

It was obvious that the house was undergoing a major redecoration. There were workmen, painters, carpenters, decorators and designers wandering around or working busily. All of them were oblivious to Frank's presence.

The character of the rooms seemed to change. The deeper he ambled into the house the smaller and more human the rooms became, less formal, more welcoming, lived-in. The further he went into the house, the nearer he drew to the sound of music. It was faint at first but grew in intensity.

His path led him into a tiled room, warm California sunlight pouring through tall french doors. The wall facing the doors was set with shelves containing the trophies of Rachel Marron's career, milestones along her rise to stardom. There was a Tony Award for Marron's first – and so far only – foray on to the Broadway stage. There were three Grammies and a slew of gold and platinum records, statuettes and plaques from organizations all over the country and the world.

The honors didn't interest Frank as much as the photographs that were also on the shelves and decorating the walls. There were dozens, most of them official pictures of Rachel Marron accepting the awards so prominently displayed with a variety of VIPs and other stars. There was one that was different. It showed Rachel Marron and a little boy – he couldn't have been more than seven – and unlike the other posed and faintly stilted pictures, this one was relaxed and easy. Mother and son were goofing off for the camera, their smiles wide, happy and unforced. The affection between them was obvious and effortless. Scrawled in a childish hand in a corner of the picture were the words: 'To Rachel Marron, my biggest fan, love Fletcher.'

Farmer smiled. He imagined that if Rachel Marron could have only one of the trophies on the shelf, if she was forced to choose, this playful photograph would take precedence over the Grammies, the Tony and the gold and platinum discs.

The music stopped abruptly.

Farmer crossed to the french doors and looked out. A rolling lawn ran down to the swimming pool. A small boy, the boy in the photograph, was crouched at the water's edge, a remote control in his hands. He was controlling a foot-long model of a 36-foot Tiara speedboat as it curved across the placid blue water. Fletcher was watching the boat intently. A nanny sat on a limestone bench a few yards away looking up from her embroidery every few minutes, as if checking to see that her charge had not fallen into the pool and drowned.

The music had started again, louder this time, with a heavy bass musical beat. It was another Rachel Marron tune, but this was an up-tempo number, bouncy and lively. He followed the sound into the next room.

It was some sort of family room, a large, comfortable

place with immense modular couches, a professional size bar, a wall of stereo gear and a projection booth.

The room was packed with people and video equipment. The young men and women in the middle of the room were dressed in sweats or tights, dancers practicing steps and routines under the direction of a choreographer. The bright sunlight streaming through the windows threw them into sharp relief against a glass brick wall at the far end of the room. A video cameraman circled, taping the rehearsal with the camera slung over his shoulder, the images he captured appearing on the large screen television on one wall.

The room was a nest of activity. Over there, a pretty black girl was being pinned into a costume, a living dummy for the costume Rachel Marron would wear in the video. Technicians were attending to the mass of video and playback gear. Grips adjusted lights and props, self-important young women, the production assistants, frowned over clipboards and talked into cordless phones. There were people everywhere, lazing on a series of high-backed couches, and it seemed that if you didn't have a specific duty in the Marron organization, you were required to stand around, smoke cigarettes, talk and laugh loudly.

As usual, no one paid any attention to Frank. He settled in a comfortable swivel stool in front of the bar and surveyed the shifting, barely controlled chaos. Out of the crowd appeared Devaney who waved and started to make his way across the room.

Frank acknowledged the greeting but his eyes were fixed on another man, a big guy, his muscles bulging in a tight white shirt, his twenty-inch neck barely encircled by the collar. His role was obvious. This hunk, this side of beef, was Security.

He had seen Frank too and had lumbered to his feet,

a scowl on his face. Devaney saw him and waved him off. 'Nothing to worry about, Tony. He's supposed to be here.'

The guy Devaney called Tony nodded and sat down again, taking a place next to another young black woman. She was not dressed as a dancer and seemed to have little interest in the scene before her. She wasn't bored or blasé; it was just that nothing out of the ordinary was going on. She looked a lot like Rachel Marron herself and she was about the same age, a little older, perhaps. You didn't have to be as astute as Frank Farmer to peg her as a relative – sister? cousin? – of the great star herself. Next to her was another, older man, talking into a cordless phone. He had a pompous, self-important air about him.

The focus of the room, though, seemed to be a deep couch set in the center of all the activity at the front of the room. The back of the piece of furniture was so tall that Frank could not see over into it, but he could guess who was sitting there. Every few seconds a PA or a secretary scurried over to the couch, respect written on her face.

The music stopped and the dancers froze in place.

'Playback, everybody!' It was the voice of the director in the control room. The images on the large screen jerked into rewind and the routine played out in reverse.

From the couch, Frank heard Rachel Marron laugh and clap. 'Rory!' she shouted at the choreographer. 'Come here, sugar. That's gonna be great. I love it . . .' All Frank could see of the woman were her arms and hands raised above the high back of the sofa.

Devaney tried to get Rachel's attention. 'Rachel, there's someone –'

'Nicki?' called Rachel, ignoring him. The woman Frank took to be a relative perked up.

'Yeah?'

'Nicki, how'd you like the number? You like the end routine? Did it play for you?'

'It was just great,' said Nicki enthusiastically.

Devaney tried again. 'Rachel, I'd like you to –'

The director's voice boomed out of one of the speakers. 'Rachel? You wanna see it back from the beginning or just the ending?'

'I wanna see it all,' shouted Rachel. 'Tony? I'll bet Tony loved it.'

Tony flicked a hand dismissively, as if waving away the video. 'Ehhh,' he said. Tony glanced over at Frank when he spoke. Farmer figured this was part of the tough-guy image. It was his way of saying that he couldn't be intimidated, not even by the boss.

'Ehhh?' said the choreographer. 'I work my butt off and all I get is an "ehhh"?'

'Don't worry, Rory,' said Rachel, smoothing the choreographer's ruffled feathers. 'That's just Tony. Tony doesn't appreciate great art.'

The girl who had been pinned into the costume edged into the star circle, elbowing Bill Devaney to one side a bit. 'What do you think, Rachel?' The girl struck a little pose. 'You like?'

Devaney broke in. 'Rachel, Frank Farmer is –'

Rachel Marron was casting a cool, critical eye over the costume, as if weighing the pros and cons of the get-up. 'Hey, Devaney,' she said. She did not take her eyes off the costume. 'You think this is me?'

Bill Devaney did not even bother to look, knowing exactly how much his opinion counted for in matters like these. 'Yeah, it's terrific ... Rachel,' he added quickly, 'Frank Farmer is here.' He nodded in Farmer's direction. All eyes, except for Rachel's, traveled to where Frank sat.

'Who's here?' asked Rachel.

'Frank Farmer.'

Rachel's only response was a blank stare.

'The bodyguard.'

There was a moment of silence, then Rachel's mouth was off and running again. 'I think Rory should be my bodyguard. Now, about this costume. Turn around so I can see that back again.'

Bill Devaney had made a very successful career out of handling highly strung, self-absorbed stars, particularly Rachel Marron. He had been there right from the beginning and understood her. Devaney knew exactly when to go along with Rachel's nonsense and when it was time to be firm.

'Rachel, raise your butt up out of that chair and meet this man.'

Rachel knew that there was no dodging this particular bullet. She stood. 'Well, I'm up.' She looked across the room at Frank.

'You want to get in here, Frank?' Devaney called.

Frank nodded, his face betraying nothing. But inside, he was thinking: *This is why I don't do celebrities*. There was more protocol involved in dealing with stars than with royalty, the White House and State Department diplomats. Rachel Marron would, with some coaxing, stand up for him, but he had to go to her once she was on her feet.

'Frank Farmer, Rachel Marron,' said Devaney triumphantly, as if he had managed to set up a tricky truce between two warring factions.

The two shook hands and Rachel looked him up and down, a small smile on her face. 'You don't look like a bodyguard.'

'What did you expect?' Frank asked evenly.

'I don't know.' She glanced over at Tony. He was

staring at them like a jealous husband. 'I guess I expected someone different. Tough guy maybe.'

'This is my disguise.'

Rachel almost laughed, but contented herself with a smile. 'Well,' she said, as if Farmer couldn't hear her, 'his timing is good.'

Devaney was on a roll. 'This is Nicki, Rachel's sister and personal secretary.'

'Nice to meet you, Mr Farmer.'

Devaney pointed to Tony. 'That's Tony Scibelli.' Tony nodded but made no effort to come over and shake hands.

'And over there, on the phone,' Bill Devaney pointed to the self-important man, 'that's Sy Spector, Rachel's publicist.'

Frank nodded, taking it all in.

Rachel appeared to be losing interest in Frank Farmer already. She was looking over the costume again. 'I don't think the back is right . . .'

'Can we get you something, Frank?' asked Devaney. 'A drink?'

'Orange juice.'

This seemed to rekindle a little interest. 'Straight?' said Rachel with a little smirk. 'Nicki, get the man an orange juice.'

'Rachel, it's time for another run-through,' shouted Rory.

'I'll be with you in a second, Rory.' She sat down on the couch and patted the space next to her, inviting Frank to sit as well. 'Listen,' she said earnestly, as if suddenly Farmer was the most important person in the room. 'I think there might have been a misunderstanding here. This whole thing is Bill's idea . . . This sudden obsession with protecting me. Tony has always handled my security and we've done just fine.' She smiled pleasantly, as if she had explained everything.

Sy Spector was edging into the circle around the star, his cordless phone still glued to his ear. 'Yes, I'll hold, but not for long . . .'

Rory was getting antsy. 'Rachel, you want to run through your steps before we go again?'

'I'll be with you in a second,' said Rachel, distractedly.

Nicki returned with a tall glass of cold, freshly squeezed orange juice. 'I think Bill's right, Rachel. It's time you took more precautions. It makes sense.' She was speaking to Rachel, but she was looking at Frank.

Sy Spector put one hand over the mouthpiece of the phone. 'Nicki, I'm sure Mr Farmer would tell you that the number of nuts writing fan letters jumps every time Rachel is on the cover of a magazine.'

Devaney shook his head. 'Not the way it's been recently. Not like this.'

An assistant thrust herself into the knot, handing a sheaf of papers to Rachel. There were phone messages, letters, documents. Rachel took the proffered pen and started leafing through the papers, signing those that required a signature. She frowned at one of the pink message slips. 'Who was this?'

'Oh,' said the assistant. 'That was Clive's office. They called three times already.'

'Rachel,' cautioned Devaney, 'let's stick to the subject.'

'Relax, guys,' she said. The irritation in her voice was plain. 'I said I'd do it. You see what I'm dealing with here?' She waved the papers, gesturing all around the room, at the dancers, the video technicians, the choreographer. 'I'm willing to go along, as long as we all understand each other. I'm not going to let this alter my life one little bit.'

'Honey,' insisted Devaney, 'that's not going to be a problem.' He turned to Frank. 'You see, Frank, we speak our mind here. And Rachel runs a very informal household – we're all on a first-name basis . . .'

If this was supposed to reassure Frank, he did not show it. Sy Spector finished his phone call and turned off the portable phone and jumped into the conversation. '*And* I'm sure you'll blend in just fine,' he said with phoney heartiness. 'You can select whatever alarm systems you want for the house. Some kind of improved security at the gate. Is there anything else you want, Rachel?'

Rachel stood and started wandering over toward Rory and his dancers. Frank looked at Devaney. Devaney looked worried. He didn't like the direction things were taking.

Rachel spoke over her shoulder. 'I think I'm safe when I'm here in the house, so I guess the main thing will be when I go out. Tony will be able to fill you in on all that. You two will have to work something out. Got that, Tony?'

'Got it, Rachel.'

'But I don't want both of you falling over me everywhere I go. The most important thing is this – I will not allow Fletcher to be affected by this thing.'

Sy Spector was already punching a new number into his telephone. 'I was just going to cover that. We'll have to tell the child you have some other function . . .'

'Yeah, that's right. I don't want him to think he's in prison. So the house and grounds must not be altered in any way. He shouldn't be aware that you're here. Is that clear?'

Frank looked at her for a full five seconds, then shot a quick glance at Devaney. 'Miss Marron . . .'

'Rachel.'

'You're absolutely right.'

'I am?'

'Yes, there *has* been a misunderstanding here.'

Rachel Marron looked triumphant. Her eyes flashed on her circle of advisers and flunkies. 'See! Told you.'

'So,' said Frank smoothly, 'if you'll show me the quickest way out, we'll save each other a lot of trouble.' He was already on his way, heading for the sliding glass doors that led outside.

'The fastest way is by the pool,' said Tony.

'Shut up, Tony,' Devaney snapped at the big man.

'It was nice meeting you all,' said Frank at the door.

'Farmer!' yelled Devaney. 'Would you wait a minute?'

'Bill,' grumbled Sy Spector. 'I don't think we should be *begging* this guy for his services.'

Devaney shot the publicist a dirty look. 'Sy, I'm handling this.' He hurried after the bodyguard, catching him on the slope above the pool. Fletcher and his nanny were still down there, the electric model boat zooming across the placid surface of the swimming pool.

'Farmer, will you wait a minute?' He touched Frank on the shoulder. 'Please.' Farmer didn't stop. 'I should have told you more,' said Devaney, talking fast. 'I'm sorry about that but I was afraid she wouldn't go through with it. I thought I would bring you together, let the two of you work it out, come to an understanding.'

'We did,' said Frank Farmer curtly.

'Look, you don't work with celebrities normally –'

'You see the reason?' said Frank gruffly.

Devaney nodded vigorously. 'I agree, but that's just how they are. They all are. It's just an act. They act *on* stage, they act *off* stage.'

Fletcher, down by the pool, was looking up the green slope toward the house, staring curiously at the two men. He had turned off the remote control and the model boat was just gliding across the water.

Devaney was doing everything he could to slow down Frank's hasty departure. 'She's not a bad person, and whether she knows it or not, she needs you.'

Frank Farmer raised his eyebrows. 'That may be, but . . .' He shrugged and kept walking.

'Please,' begged Devaney. 'You've come this far. Would you wait here for one minute? I want to show you something. Please, Farmer.'

Frank stopped and turned, seeming resigned to staying on the grounds of the estate for just five more minutes.

'Okay, okay,' said Devaney, backing away from Frank like a man afraid that his words would provoke an attack. 'Just stay right there and I'll be back in a minute. Please.' He turned and hurried back toward the house.

Frank Farmer watched him go, and the instant Devaney disappeared inside the bodyguard started walking again, heading for his car and a return to his quiet, discreet world.

CHAPTER FOUR

Frank was anxious to get out of there, but found his path blocked by an obstacle he couldn't quite get around, that barely came up to his belt buckle. Seven-year-old Fletcher, all four feet of him, stood on the path between Frank and the exit, the remote control box in his tiny hands.

'Hi,' said Fletcher.

'Hi,' said Frank.

'How are you today?'

'All right,' lied Frank. 'How 'bout yourself?' He glanced over his shoulder. Devaney would be back in a matter of seconds and then he would be trapped.

'Oh, I'm fine.' It seemed to Frank that in all the hustle and bustle of the Marron household no one was delegated to pay much attention to Fletcher. The little boy seemed delighted to have someone to talk to. 'Do you like boats?'

Frank smiled. 'No. I don't like boats.'

Fletcher's eyes grew wide. How could anyone not like boats? 'You don't! Why not?'

Frank shook his head. 'Oh, I don't know . . . Just one of those things, I guess. I can't explain it.'

Fletcher didn't believe this for a second. His eyes narrowed. 'Sure you do, but you don't want to tell me.'

Frank considered this for a moment, looking at the little boy with respect. He crouched down until he was eye to eye with Fletcher. 'You know, you're a smart kid.'

Fletcher nodded. Frank's observation was nothing more than the truth and the child knew it.

'I'll tell you why I hate boats,' said Frank. 'One time I was stuck on a boat with some people for four months.'

'Wow! Were you in a lifeboat?'

Frank shook his head. 'Nope. A big white yacht. Do you know what a yacht is?'

Fletcher nodded. 'Yeah. My mom rented this huge yacht once and we took a trip. It was great. Everyone threw up except me. I love boats. Any kind of boat. Big ones, little ones. I don't care.'

'Well, nobody is perfect.' Frank stood up again and glanced toward the house. There was no sign of Devaney. Maybe he could still get out of there without being pursued.

Fletcher was staring up at him, squinting slightly, the sun in his eyes. 'You're the bodyguard, aren't you?'

The kid was full of surprises. 'What do you know about it?'

'I've got ears,' said Fletcher simply.

'I'll remember that,' said Frank. And he meant it. Adults always made the mistake of thinking that they spoke a different language, a patois that children couldn't understand. Kids could be as discreet and as sensitive as well-placed surveillance microphones.

'Farmer! I want you to see this.' Devaney was emerging from the house, relieved to see that Frank had waited for him. He was carrying a bulging manila file, but when he caught sight of the little boy he lowered his arm, holding the dossier casually at his side, as if suddenly the folder was no big deal. Frank saw Fletcher eyeing the file curiously.

'How are you, Fletch?'

'Fine.'

'Good. Frank, why don't we go over and sit on the patio? Catch you later, Fletch.'

'Uh-huh. It was nice meeting you, Frank,' the little boy said solemnly.

'Likewise.'

Fletcher stared after them a moment, then trotted back to the pool and his boat.

In the course of Frank Farmer's career as a bodyguard he had seen dozens of files like the one Devaney laid open in front of him on the glass-topped patio table. It was a collection of crank letters. Some were long, rambling missives written in an unsteady hand on cheap paper. Others were immaculately typed. Others yet were assembled from cut-out letters. All were threatening.

The menaces took various forms. Some were direct, to the point, advising Rachel Marron to prepare to die. Others were violently obscene, specifying in hateful detail just what the author of the letter would do to Rachel prior to killing her. To Frank, though, the most disturbing were the letters that promised to get not only Rachel but her son as well. He glanced over to the pool, as if reassuring himself that Fletcher was still there.

'This is just the batch we've collected in the last six months,' said Devaney.

'Have you ever tried having these professionally assessed?'

Devaney shook his head. 'What's to assess? These people are sick.'

Frank nodded. 'Yes, but are they sick *and* dangerous?'

He was going through the letters, carefully turning the pages holding just a corner of each letter between his thumb and index finger. It was nothing more than a habit – these papers had been handled by so many people it would be impossible to get any kind of fingerprint lift from them.

Sy Spector wandered on to the patio, sucking on an ice-cream cone. He leaned over Frank Farmer's shoulder, peering nonchalantly at the letters as Frank scanned each one then assigned it to a particular pile.

'Devaney says you were in the Secret Service,' he said, slurping down a little ice cream.

Frank nodded, concentrating on the letters.

'Ever guard the main man?'

'I was two years with Carter and four years with Reagan.'

'Reagan got shot,' said Spector.

'Not on my shift.'

Sy Spector guffawed. 'That's good.'

Farmer did not look up from his task. He paused to read one letter and smiled. 'This one is from a little old lady in Akron. She's written to everybody I've ever worked for. Always the same story: I love you so much, I'm going to kill you. She's harmless.'

'So we can rule out one psycho,' said Devaney, 'but there are fifty, sixty letters there.'

'It's not as bad as that. At first glance, these don't bother me.' He placed his hand on one pile. 'But keep them. You never know.' There was one letter separate from the others. It was a meticulously neat message, fastidiously pasted down.

Devaney paled slightly when he saw the letter that Farmer had singled out. MARRON BITCH – YOU HAVE EVERYTHING. I HAVE NOTHING. THE TIME TO DIE IS COMING.

'You think it could be the same guy? The one who rigged the doll?'

Frank shrugged. 'I don't know. Hard to tell. Did you tell Miss Marron about it? Does she know about the doll?'

Sy Spector and Bill Devaney exchanged glances. Devaney grimaced as he did so. Frank Farmer sensed that he had touched a nerve, that this was a sore point between the two men.

Spector cleared his throat. 'We said there'd been some electrical problem while she was on the stage. Short circuit or something like that.'

'So she's not really aware of the danger she's in?' Farmer didn't show it, but he was amazed.

'Look,' said Spector defensively, 'she doesn't need that kind of worry right now. It would upset her.'

'She'd be more upset if she had gotten blown up,' grumbled Devaney.

'Bill . . .'

Frank Farmer moved quickly to prevent the re-opening of an old argument. It would prove nothing and it would waste time. 'What about the police? Did you go to them after the incident with the doll?' His eyes darted back to the pool, to Fletcher and his model speedboat.

'There was no reason to go to the police,' said Spector. 'No one got hurt.'

Frank raised an eyebrow. 'What about the chauffeur?'

'It was not serious, a scratch. It was nothing. Only our people were there.'

Frank turned and watched Fletcher again, wondering what Spector's attitude would have been if Fletcher had been backstage that night. He suspected that it wouldn't have been much different.

Devaney was watching Frank closely. Farmer maintained a pretty good poker face, but Devaney could see that he was wavering. With a little luck and a little more pressure he might be able to hook him. 'Sy,' he said, 'I think we should show Frank the room.'

The room sounded ominous, but at first glance it wasn't. It was, in fact, a bedroom, a garish riot of pink satin and floor-to-ceiling mirrors. The furniture was over-upholstered, white and gilt faux-Louis XIV, the centerpiece being an extravagantly draped curtain bed. The room was about the size of a tennis court. Frank thought that he would sink to his knees in the thick carpet.

'Is this her bedroom?' asked Frank. Gaudy though the room may have been, it was immaculately clean, every item in place, perfectly neat, with no sign of human habitation.

'Yes,' said Spector.

Devaney shot him an angry glance. 'Sy, we have to be upfront about this. We're not getting anywhere lying to Frank. This isn't her bedroom. Rachel sleeps in a room next to Fletcher's down the hall.'

'Then what's this?'

'Sy had this done for a magazine layout,' Devaney said with distaste.

'"Superstars in their Boudoirs",' said Sy Spector proudly. 'Did you happen to see it?'

Frank shook his head. 'No, I guess I missed that.'

'Rachel never liked it,' said Devaney.

'She didn't have to like it,' growled Spector. 'You guys just don't understand publicity.'

Devaney laid the letter on the bed. 'We found the letter here.'

'Here? Here on the bed? Someone was in here?'

Devaney sighed heavily. 'Somebody broke in and . . . somebody broke in and masturbated on the bed.'

'And let me guess – she doesn't know about this either, right?'

Devaney shook his head. 'No, I'm afraid not.'

'Tell her?' said Spector in alarm. 'Are you kidding? This would really freak her out.'

'What do you think, Frank?'

Farmer folded his arms across his chest. 'Someone penetrates the house, gets upstairs and jerks off on the bed . . . I'd say that qualifies as a problem,' he said evenly.

'What kind of problem?'

Spector was getting more and more agitated. 'Oh, fuck! We don't need this now.'

'This house is wide open,' said Frank matter-of-factly.

'Excuse me? What the hell does that mean?' demanded Spector. 'We have security.'

'This house is wide open and you people have no clue what real security is or what it takes to achieve it.'

Devaney didn't care how much he annoyed Spector. It was Farmer he needed right now. 'Frank,' he said sincerely, 'I totally respect what you're telling me. Tell me how you want to work and I'll accommodate you.'

'Oh, for Christ's sake,' said Spector testily.

'Look, I can't protect her. I won't be responsible for her safety if she doesn't know what's going on.'

'Frank, I'll talk to her, I'll make her understand. I can do that.'

'No,' snapped Spector. 'I'll talk to her.' He strode out of the room in a huff.

Devaney waited until Sy Spector was out of earshot. 'Don't worry about Sy, Frank. He'll get used to the idea. He's not a problem.'

'I hope not,' murmured Frank Farmer.

'Don't worry about it.' Devaney clapped him on the back. 'You bring your suitcase? I'll walk you to your car.'

Henry had finished washing the Jaguar and was working on the Cadillac limousine, hosing it down. He watched curiously as Devaney and Frank emerged from the house.

'. . . Rachel won't give you any static, Frank. You've got my word on that.'

'*Sure* she will,' scoffed Frank.

Devaney smiled. 'So what job is perfect? You're a bodyguard, aren't you?'

'Yeah,' said Frank.

'Henry! I want you to take Frank up to his room.'

'Devaney,' said Frank, 'there's just one thing I want you to know.'

'Anything. Anything you want, Frank.' Bill Devaney was elated at having snagged Frank Farmer. He wanted to put all security problems behind him.

'It's very simple.' Frank kept his voice low. 'If you ever lie to me again, I'll take you apart.'

Devaney's face fell. 'Oh.'

Out of consideration for Henry's injured hand, Frank Farmer carried his own bag to the room assigned to him. The room was comfortably furnished, but it had all the soul of a hotel room. It didn't matter to Frank what the room was like. He knew he wouldn't be spending all that much time there – it would be little more than a place to sleep and change his clothes.

Henry leaned against the door, watching as Frank unpacked his battered suitcase.

'Can I ask you a question?'

Frank shoved some shirts into a dresser drawer. 'Sure.'

'Why did you say your name was Edison?'

'I wanted to see how hard it was to get in,' said Frank.

'And it wasn't hard, was it?' Unconsciously, Henry flexed the muscles in his injured arm, easing the pain in his hand.

Frank noticed the young man's discomfort. He pulled a tube of ointment from his suitcase and tossed it to the chauffeur. 'Put this on your arm. It'll help the ache.'

'Thanks.' Henry was noncommittal, as if not quite sure of Frank. Maybe he would turn out to be the enemy.

'I'll bet you can fill up a whole day just washing the cars and driving Rachel Marron around town.'

Henry shrugged. 'That's my job.'

'We're adding to your duties,' said Frank matter-of-factly.

'Huh?'

'You're my new assistant.' Farmer pulled three heavy boxes of 9-millimeter ammunition from his suitcase and stashed them in the drawer of the night table next to the bed.

Henry was startled. 'Says who?'

Frank looked the young man square in the eye. 'Henry, I've spent a lot of time guarding people all over the world and I've found one thing to be true.'

'Yeah? What would that be?'

'You can take this to the bank, Henry. Trust me on this. No matter how incompetent the assassins, no matter how much they miss the target, there's one person who always gets hit.'

'Really? Who?'

Frank smiled. 'The cocky black chauffeur.'

CHAPTER FIVE

Frank Farmer used his *carte blanche* to make changes in the Marron estate, surveying the property as if he were a general fortifying a citadel against a long siege. With Henry as aide-de-camp taking notes, the two men tramped through every inch of the grounds, looking for weak points in the perimeter. There were lots of them.

The tall, ragged hedge that separated the estate from the neighboring property was the first problem that had to be addressed. The greenery was pretty, but it was easy to penetrate and there were a hundred hiding places in the dark shrubbery.

'It's got to go,' said Frank firmly.

'And be replaced with what?' asked Henry sceptically.

'An electric fence.'

Henry laughed. 'Hey, Frank, this is Bel Air, man. You can't put up a big electric fence. You know who lives next door?'

'No. Who?'

Henry mentioned a movie star, a name so big that even Frank Farmer had heard of him.

'Oh.' Farmer frowned.

'I don't think he's gonna appreciate you putting up a fence that looks like it should be around a federal pen.'

'No, I guess not.' Frank considered this for a moment. 'Okay, this is what we'll do. Get the hedge trimmed and cut down to eight feet.'

Henry scribbled on his pad. 'Uh-huh.'

'Then we'll put the fence inside the perimeter to a height of nine feet. Think the superstar next door will go for that? He'll only see twelve inches of the fence.'

Henry considered this a moment. 'Well, his last two movies were dogs and Rachel is getting to be the bigger star. If she get's herself nominated, then he'll realize who's got the power.' Henry nodded. 'Yeah, I think we can get away with that much fence showing.'

Frank Farmer looked at his assistant, amazement showing plainly in his face. He shook his head slowly. 'Show business,' he said.

Frank chose eight points on the front lawn for surveillance camera poles, discreet columns topped by ever vigilant television cameras that would sweep the lawns and gardens with an electronic eye. Each view would interlock, eliminating blind spots and sending pictures back to two points: to a security room inside the house itself and to a solid brick guard house Frank Farmer wanted to erect just inside the gate.

'That reminds me,' said Frank. 'New gates. New gate posts. New intercom.'

'Got it,' said Henry.

'Now let's check out the house.'

The house was a sieve, exterior doors everywhere leading from the grounds into the heart of the building. Short of bricking up entire doors, there was little Frank could do except order a new alarm system and new hard-to-pick locks.

'Is there a bathroom off Miss Marron's bedroom? I mean her *real* bedroom?'

'Yeah.'

'Okay. I want a new door, a steel reinforced door for that bathroom. Bars on the windows . . .'

'Uh-huh.'

'There a telephone in there?'

'No, I don't think so.'

'Put one in. Separate line, separate switching box. Then get the alarm company to put a remote-controlled panic button in there.'

'All this for a bathroom?' asked Henry incredulously.

'It's not just a bathroom anymore,' said Frank with a slight smile.

'No? What is it?'

'LPR,' said Farmer.

'And what might that stand for?'

'Last point of refuge. If everything else fails, Miss Marron is supposed to get in that bathroom, lock herself in, hit the panic button and wait until help shows up. If the phone line isn't cut, then she can communicate with the outside world. If it is –' Frank shrugged.

Henry laughed. 'What are you expecting? Airborne? Commandos? The Iraqis? Or just plain good old-fashioned nuclear war?'

'Just do it, Henry. Now.'

'What are you going to do?'

'I'm going to take a look at the pool and the pool house.'

'Wait. Let me guess. You're going to put piranhas in the pool, piranhas *and* crocodiles. No. I got it. You're going to fill it with acid. Acid and piranhas and crocodiles.'

Frank smiled. 'Remember what I told you about the cocky black chauffeur, Henry?'

Henry went off to make the calls, laughing to himself.

The pool house was about five hundred yards from the

house, a vaguely Spanish-looking building of white stucco topped by a red tile roof. Frank could more or less guess what was inside: changing rooms, showers, a couple of rooms filled with old lawn furniture and pool toys.

As he neared the building, though, he was surprised to hear music coming from within. On a low table was a big black sound system, the five-CD turntable loaded with hip-hop. The music that blared from the powerful speaker was loud and fast, driven by a quick, deep bass beat bursting with energy. Next to the player was a big color TV set tuned to Cable News Network, the sound turned off.

Frank peered through the glass doors that led out to the pool deck. A small room had been fitted out with a wall of mirrors and a ballet barre. Nicki stood in the middle of the room wearing a leotard that clung to her body like a second skin, and she was doing some stretching exercises, warming up for what promised to be a strenuous aerobic workout.

She caught sight of Frank, smiled and waved him in. He tried to push open the door but found that the path was blocked by a mountain of sleeping dog, a giant St Bernard, the size of a couch.

Frank paused. He had a healthy respect for large dogs – he was reminded of the old proverb: a dog is just a dog until he growls – then he is *Mister* Dog.

'He won't bite.' Nicki had to shout to make herself heard over the music.

Frank pushed the door back with some difficulty, sliding the big dog across the floor. Not only did the dog not bite, it didn't even bother to wake up.

'Unusual tactic for a guard dog,' he shouted. 'But effective.'

Nicki picked up a remote control clicker, turned down the music and laughed. 'Guard dog? Hannibal doesn't have a mean bone in his body.'

At the sound of his name, the St Bernard opened one eye, discovered nothing of interest, gave a titanic, skull-stretching yawn and went back to sleep.

'Don't let me disturb you,' said Frank. 'I'm just looking around.'

She beckoned him into the room. 'You can look around all you like.'

'I don't think that will be necessary.' He turned to go. 'I'm sorry I bothered you.'

'That's all right. It's an excuse to avoid exercising.'

'You don't like it?'

'I do it,' said Nicki with a good-natured laugh, 'but nothing says I have to like it.'

'I know the –'

'Ssh,' she said quickly, holding up her hand like a cop stopping traffic. She pointed the remote control at the TV set and brought the sound up. 'Martin Grove,' she said. '*Showbiz Today*.'

Martin Grove, the Cable News Network entertainment reporter, was one of the more powerful showbusiness journalists in the city, his prognostications followed breathlessly by thousands of people in 'the industry'.

'It's Oscar time again, folks, and with Academy members marking their ballots today for this year's nominations, some canny tipsters in Vegas have announced their picks for the awards.'

'Vegas?' said Frank Farmer. 'People bet on the Academy Awards?'

Nicki didn't answer. She stood absolutely still as if movement would have made a noise.

'Echoing the prevailing buzz in Hollywood, the Las

Vegas Hilton is gambling on one sure thing at least. Newcomer Rachel Marron is tipped at three to one to lead this year's Best Actress runners.'

'Yeah!' said Nicki with a broad smile. She punched a fist in the air.

Grove continued over a still photograph of Rachel holding the Grammy she had won the year before. 'The sultry singer made a notable acting debut last fall in *Queen of the Night*, singing the hit song "I Have Nothing". The lady may end up eating those words if she takes home that statuette come March 20th ... Teen heartthrob Luke Perry, star of Fox's –'

Nicki snapped off the sound. 'She's going to get nominated and she's going to win. You can bet on that.'

'Looks like some people are doing just that.'

'Smart money.'

Nicki aimed the remote control at the CD player and brought the music up again, but not too loud.

'Anyone else work out here?' Frank asked.

Nicki shook her head. 'Nope. I guess this is my private place. I'm just about the only one who works out around here.'

There was little decoration in the room, just some photographs on the whitewashed wall. He glanced at them. They were all of Nicki Marron, taken at various stages of her life. There were photographs of her on stage, a little girl, obviously in a school play.

'*Raisin in the Sun*,' she said. Her laugh was slightly embarrassed, self-conscious. 'Mrs Parker's eighth-grade class.' She flicked her hand toward the photographs. 'My own ego wall,' she said dismissively. 'No platinum records.'

'Not yet.'

'Not *ever*,' said Nicki emphatically.

Frank studied one of the pictures, a photograph

49

taken later in life – Nicki looked as if she was about seventeen or eighteen – fronting a band. She was clutching a microphone, and even in a still, silent picture you could tell she was singing her heart out.

The next photograph on the wall showed two girls fronting the band.

'You and Rachel?' Frank asked.

Nicki shrugged. 'When I was a kid, I put a little band together. We played high-school dances, stuff like that. Then Rachel joined the act.' Nicki laughed. 'As you can imagine, she was quite a little entertainer. Even back then she had a way of stopping the show.'

'So?'

'So I kind of quit. Professionally, anyway.'

'You never went back?'

'It was pretty obvious who the star in our family was.' Nicki spoke without bitterness, not a trace of envy or resentment in her voice. Her words were just a simple statement of fact, but her smile was rueful, tinged with a dash of regret.

Henry tapped at the glass doors. 'All done, Frank,' he said. 'Work begins tomorrow. You have any idea how much this is going to cost? Rachel *better* win that Oscar so she can afford all this protection.'

'It's a lot cheaper than getting killed,' said Nicki seriously.

Frank smiled. 'I'm glad someone is on my side. C'mon, Henry. Time to go.'

'Where now?'

'The garage.'

'What for?'

'You'll see.'

'Catch you later, Nicki,' called Henry. But she didn't hear him. She had already boosted the music back up to ear-splitting volume.

★

'Now what's the matter with the garage?' asked Henry as the two men climbed the grassy slope up to the house.

'It's not the garage,' said Frank. 'It's what's in the garage.'

'The cars?'

Frank Farmer nodded. 'The cars.'

'You going to armor-plate them?'

Frank paused for a moment as if considering the idea. He dismissed it. 'No, that's probably not necessary, but I think we ought to eliminate any hints.'

'Hints? Hints of what?'

'I don't want anyone on the street to be able to look at the cars and know who owns them.'

Henry leaned into the side door of the garage and hit the button that activated the electric garage opener. 'I don't think there's anything here you would call a hint.'

The doors rattled open, revealing the tail ends of the three Marron limousines. 'No?' said Frank. 'How about that?' He pointed to the license plate of the big Cadillac limousine. The plate read: Rachel 2.

'Or that?' The plate of the dove-gray Mercedes read: Rachel 3.

Frank shook his head over the third car. It was the large Jaguar XKE, a car much favored with the Hollywood élite – except this one was painted an outrageous, screaming bright pink. The license tag on this one read: Rachel 1.

'I guess I'd call those hints,' said Henry, laughing.

Frank popped the hood of the Jag and then leaned into the engine. A moment later he emerged with the distributor in his hand.

'Hey! That's Rachel's favorite car!'

Farmer shrugged, the gesture saying, loud and clear,

'Too bad.' 'This one can't be driven at all,' he decreed. 'And get new plates for the others too.'

Henry scribbled a note. 'Yes, boss.'

Over the next few days construction crews worked twelve-hour shifts, scrambling to build all the security improvements Frank Farmer had asked for. The electric fence went up in record time, and within a week the electronic surveillance devices were in place.

Frank Farmer personally interviewed the uniformed security people who would man the gate and the television monitors. Protection service is a big, sophisticated business in the richer parts of Los Angeles, and there was no shortage of firms willing to provide exactly the personnel required – guards were polygraphed and questioned, quizzed about drug and alcohol use, even driving records. Frank pronounced himself pleased with the men he hired, but he knew better than to expect anything heroic from the guards. When you came right down to it, security guards were just rent-a-cops, who would do no more than was warranted by the twelve bucks an hour they received in pay. People didn't get themselves killed for four hundred and eighty dollars a week, plus overtime.

Devaney groaned about the cost of all this, Rachel Marron grumbled about the inconvenience and the disfigurement of her property, Frank fretted about the the quality of the work. Only one person was delighted with the upheaval: Fletcher.

For a couple of days, the little boy abandoned his model boats to watch the construction of gates and walls, marveling at the thundering behemoth of a bulldozer that snorted around the property, uprooting trees and effortlessly knocking down walls.

When destruction ceased to be interesting, he liked

to watch as Frank Farmer gave Henry lessons in defensive driving. The big Cadillac limo would come thundering down the long drive, picking up speed, then suddenly Henry swung the wheel hard right, locking it, slamming on the brakes and flooring the gas pedal at the same time. As the tires shrieked like banshees, the huge car careened to the right and pivoted on the locked brakes, swinging the vehicle around in a cloud of dust. In seconds the Caddy had turned through 180 degrees, facing back the way it came.

Henry climbed out of the car and wiped his brow. 'Whew. That was fun!'

'Frank!' shouted Fletcher. 'Teach me how to do that!'

The dust was still settling around the car. 'Hey, Frank, can I try it again?'

'Sure. In a minute . . .' Farmer wasn't paying attention. He was gazing out into the street. A few hundred yards down Waverly Lane the snub prow of the black Toyota 4 × 4 protruded from a side street. Fletcher followed the line of his stare.

Very slowly, the car turned in a wide U-turn and drove sedately away from the mansion.

The screaming brakes of the limousine had drawn Rachel out on to the balcony that encircled the upper storey of her house. She stood there a moment, inspecting the scene before her: the cloud of settling dust, the workmen and their power tools, the rumbling bulldozer. In the middle of it all was her tiny son. The chance of catastrophe seemed enormous – but most of all, she didn't like the idea of her little boy befriending the bodyguard.

She cupped her hands around her mouth. 'Fletcher! C'mon! You get back in here.'

He turned and squinted into the sun, looking at his mother. 'Aww, Mom.'

'C'mon. You heard me.'

The little boy shrugged. 'Gotta go,' he said to Frank.

'You have to keep your mother happy.'

'Yeah, I guess so . . .' He started toward the house. 'I think he's got a black 4 × 4,' the little boy muttered *sotto voce*. 'Could be a Chevy. More like a Toyota. A Toyota Four-Runner.'

Frank Farmer nodded gravely, as if Fletcher was an equal, a colleague. 'I'll check it out.

CHAPTER SIX

The room was cool and dark and the only sound was the metallic slip and click as the slide projector came on, throwing a beam of hot white light on to the screen.

In the shadows behind the projector, Frank spoke. 'Okay, this is the one that we're concentrating on.'

On the screen were the cut-out letters of the carefully constructed hate note. MARRON BITCH – YOU HAVE EVERYTHING. I HAVE NOTHING. THE TIME TO DIE IS COMING.

Another voice cut through the darkness. 'Where'd you get it, Frank?' The man's voice was smooth, as if worn down from years of whiskey and cigarettes. It was Ray Court, a gray and grizzled veteran of the Secret Service. He had been guarding presidents, potentates and politicians for decades, dating back to the Kennedy administration. Court was proud of that. In the lapel of his blue suit jacket was a tiny PT 109 Boat pin, a gift from JFK himself. Court hadn't been in Dallas that day in 1963, and there had been a time when he thought that might have made a difference. Now he wasn't so sure.

'We're taking it seriously because of where we got it. They found it on her bed. Someone left it there and jerked off on the bed. A little calling card.'

There was another man in the audience. He laughed drily. 'Jeez, there are some goddamn freaks in this world, huh, Frank? Did anyone think to save the jizz stains?' This was Terry Minella, also of the Secret

Service. He was younger than Court but fast becoming as jaded as his colleague.

'Marron's people aren't trained to think that way, Terry.'

'That's too bad, we could have run a DNA scan on it. It wouldn't have given us a name and address, but at least we would have known basic info – age, race, that kind of thing.'

Ray Court spoke up. 'There's been a preliminary study on this note. Lots of work went into it. No prints. None. Nothing. Not even a partial. That doesn't happen by accident.'

'No,' agreed Frank.

'This is the one you think is tied to the doll?' asked Minella. A match flared close to his face. A second later a curl of blue cigarette smoke floated into the beam of the projector.

'That's what her manager thinks,' said Frank.

Court continued to stare at the note on the screen. 'This "I Have Nothing" business is a natural with the record and movie and all.'

'It's a nice tune, too,' put in Minella.

'Okay, Frank,' said Court. 'Let's wrap it up.'

Farmer turned off the projector and turned on the lights. The screening room in the Federal Building in downtown Los Angeles was as bare and as drab as a government facility was supposed to be. Court stood up, stretching as if the hard federal-issue chair had taxed his bad back.

'I sort of lost track of you after Washington, Frank,' he said. The old Secret Service agent ran his eye over Farmer's conservative gray pin-striped suit. Frank was not a flashy dresser, but his clothes were well cut, good quality – better than the threadbare, slightly shiny suit that Ray Court wore.

Frank was typically noncommittal. 'Yeah? Well, I've been around.'

'How's the private stuff? Taking care of yourself?'

'Fine. I'm doing okay.'

Court winked. 'Big money, I bet? Huh?'

Frank shrugged. Court and Minella exchanged knowing looks. Minella smirked.

'Shit!' Court slapped his fist into his hand. 'I knew it. It is big money. Fuck!'

'It's not that big,' said Frank with a smile.

'Yeah, sure,' said Court sceptically. 'Look, Frank, you need an assistant? I'm ready to get out.'

'You? C'mon,' said Frank, 'you'd never leave Treasury. You'll die in this job.'

'That's exactly what I'm afraid of.' Court laughed heartily. 'But seriously, Frank, I have to get out. I'm losing my number-one qualification for this job. You know what that is? An unbelievable ability to tolerate assholic behavior.'

'Have to put up with that on the outside too, Ray.'

'Not the way it is on the inside. You should see the guy we're covering now . . .'

'Senator "Hellfire Henry" Kent,' put in Terry Minella. He drew on his cigarette. 'Somebody wants to pop him. Can you imagine taking one for *him*?'

Senator Kent was the senior senator for a Bible Belt state who had an unerring instinct for annoying people. Now that Godless Communism was no longer an acceptable whipping boy, he had chosen 'the decline of family values' as his personal theme. It gave him the chance to deliver long and faintly salacious sermons on the evils of pornography, homosexuality, prostitution, unwed mothers, abortion and obscene rock and roll lyrics.

'It's not surprising someone wants him dead,

considering what the shithead's been saying.' said Court evenly. 'Plus the guy never shuts up. Shoot him and we'll all get some peace and quiet.'

Minella agreed enthusiastically. 'Yeah! Do everyone a favor . . .' The agent coughed ironically. 'As you know, Frank, we're non-political these days.'

The three men laughed easily. Frank knew exactly what was going on here. Secret Service agents considered themselves soldiers, soldiers in a vaguely defined, but none the less deadly war. It was a soldier's right to complain about his superiors, about the tasks he was ordered to carry out, but when the time came he would put aside his rancor and do his duty.

Court glanced at his watch. 'Gotta get going.'

'Me too,' said Frank.

'We'll put this stuff through Washington, Frank. Behavioral Sciences should have something in a few days.'

'Thanks.' Frank turned to go, then stopped. 'Ray?'

'Yeah?'

'Why am I getting all this cooperation?'

'Hey, it's out of the goodness of our heart, Frank.' Court grinned and patted Farmer on the shoulder.

'Yeah,' Minella chimed in. 'Rachel Marron's a citizen, a tax payer. Deserves to be protected as much as the big guy himself.'

'What's the real answer?'

'It's simple. She's a big star. Important people care about her,' said Minella.

'You know how it is, Frank,' Court added. 'Politics and show business are practically the same thing these days.'

'I guess . . .'

'By the way,' asked Minella, 'got any crowd photos we could use? See if any familiar faces show up. Can't hurt.'

'I don't know how much good that would do. She's got a clique of fans, real hard-core types. They follow her everywhere. They say they love her.'

'Yeah, love her to death.'

'I'll look around and see what they have in the files but there won't be much current.'

'Why not?' asked Minella.

'Because I'm trying to keep her away from crowds.'

Court laughed. Rachel Marron *not* drawing a crowd? 'Good luck.'

The Ivy on Main in Santa Monica was a quiet, elegant-but-casual restaurant much favored by the rich and famous in the entertainment industry. During the luncheon hour the two dozen tables in the hushed main dining room and the few tables outside on the terrace drew prominent agents, studio executives, producers, directors and, of course, the pinnacle of Hollywood aristocracy, the stars themselves.

At one o'clock on a warm afternoon, a number of world-famous names could be seen dining there, the food artfully prepared and flawlessly served. Table hopping – an Olympic sport in Hollywood – was not encouraged at the Ivy. It was not enough to *say* you were a 'close personal friend' of this star or that executive – you really had to be one to be able to greet the great as they ate their microscopic meals and drank designer water.

Just to annoy Frank, Rachel Marron had refused a choice inside table, insisting that the maître d' seat her outside on the terrace, close enough to the street to be in danger from a passer-by.

The meal, taken with Sy Spector, Nicki and some awestruck entertainment journalists from three medium-circulation newspapers from the Midwest, had been a nerve-racking experience for Farmer. It was his first time out in public with his new employer, the first time he'd got to see her in the public eye. It was also early in this investigation and he still had little idea of who he was looking for. All he could do was remain vigilant, ever on guard.

And Rachel Marron was being her most unpredictable. In contrast to other people – even people in the entertainment industry – stars had a God-given right to table hop or to summon to their presence any person they chose. Few people refused the call. There was constant traffic to and from the Marron table.

As if to annoy him further, Rachel had added to her entourage, insisting that Tony come along to assist with security. The big man dogged Farmer, getting in the way, offering advice and generally attempting to throw his considerable weight around.

When ninety minutes had passed, Sy Spector looked at his watch and spoke in a low voice to the three journalists. The luncheon interview was over. They suddenly remembered that they had appointments elsewhere, thanked Rachel profusely for her time and departed, presumably to write several weeks' worth of fawning stories telling the folks back home what Rachel Marron was 'Really Like'. Frank noticed that it was all the three writers could do to stop themselves from walking out backward, as if leaving the presence of royalty.

Rachel and Spector conferred for a few minutes more, Nicki sitting quietly next to her sister, removed from the conversation. Then they all rose and made for the exit.

It's about time, thought Frank Farmer.

It was almost as if she read the relief on his face. Rachel scanned the diners for a familiar face and, of course, found one. A middle-aged woman, a middle-level executive at one of the studios – not normally someone Rachel would have had much time for – caught the star's eye and she walked quickly to her table.

'Abby!' squealed Rachel Marron.

'Rachel!' The two women greeted each other as if they were sisters separated since birth but finally, against all odds, reunited. Each kissed the air next to the other's right cheek.

They immediately fell to whispering, like teenage girls at a school dance. Abby said something to Rachel who turned and glanced at Frank; Rachel whispered something in return and they both fell prey to fits of giggles. Then they kissed again and Rachel moved on, both having accomplished their goals. Abby had demonstrated to everyone in the room that she was somebody to be reckoned with. Rachel had managed to irritate her bodyguard further.

As an afterthought, Abby smiled at Nicki. 'Goodbye, Nicki,' she cooed. '*So* great to see you.' The phoniness in her voice was apparent and it was meant to be. It said: You may be her sister, but that doesn't make you anything more than a hanger-on.

Nicki waved and managed a smile. Frank thought she showed more grace than was actually required in the circumstances, but he was coming to admire Rachel Marron's soft-spoken sister. She was a breath of fresh air in the cloud of fakery that seemed to hover over Hollywood. It was worse than the smog.

Henry had brought the Cadillac limousine up to the front door of the restaurant. Frank slipped out of the building first, scanning the street and the parking lot, looking for trouble. He motioned his party forward, but just as Rachel Marron stepped on to the sidewalk, she found her path blocked.

'Rachel!' yelled a little girl.

Where the hell did you come from? Frank tensed.

'Hi, honey,' said Rachel, flashing the child a big smile.

The girl thrust an autograph book up toward the star. 'Can I have your autograph?' she lisped.

'Why, sure, darling. What's your name?'

'Cindy.'

As Rachel signed a long message in the little girl's book, Cindy's mother came thundering into the group. 'Oh, Rachel,' she yelped, 'I'm Cindy's mom. This is such a thrill. I'm your biggest fan, you know.' She thrust her hand into her big shoulder bag and pulled out something black. It filled her hand.

It took no more than a split second for Frank to recognize the object – it was a camera – but in that moment his heart beat increased dramatically.

'Can we get a picture?'

Rachel laughed. 'Of course. Cindy, you get right here next to me and you too, Cindy's mom. Nicki, take our picture.'

Cindy's mother linked arms with Rachel and, fixing a smile on her face, stared into the camera lens. She seemed to be trembling with excitement. The camera whirred and clicked.

'One more!' insisted Rachel. 'Nicki, take another one.'

Obediently, Nicki did as she was told, then surrendered the camera to the woman.

'There you go,' said Rachel. 'Now I want you to be on my side come Oscar night.'

'You bet, Rachel,' said the woman. 'I know you're going to win. I can feel it in my bones.'

'That's good. I'll bet you have good bones, too.' The woman shrieked with laughter, and it looked for a moment as if Rachel was inclined to stand there on the sidewalk and talk to her a little more. Frank Farmer had had enough. He pulled open the limo door and ushered his charge into the vehicle. Rachel allowed herself to be conducted away.

'I'm surprised you didn't plug them,' she whispered as she slipped into the car.

I damn near did, thought Frank. He slammed the door and then stood on the sidewalk a little longer, scanning the area. Tony was at his side, anxious to get going.

'Hey,' he said impatiently, 'let's go.'

Cindy and her mother lingered on the sidewalk. 'We met Rachel Marron,' said the woman to no one in particular. She looked a little dazed. 'Rachel Marron!'

'I said, let's go,' Tony insisted. 'We're running late.'

Frank Farmer didn't bother to look at him. 'Get in the car.'

'But –'

'Get in the car.' Tony got into the car. Frank took one more look at the area and took the right front passenger seat, squeezing Tony between him and Henry.

'Okay, Henry,' said Frank quietly. 'Let's go.'

'Yep.' Henry slipped the gear into drive and the giant car pulled out of the parking lot, smooth and slow, like a yacht putting out to sea.

Tony was steaming with anger. He spoke in a whisper, but he could not hide his fury. 'Let me set you straight on a few things, Farmer,' he muttered angrily.

Frank's eyes were locked on the mirror mounted on his door, watching the lane of traffic to the right. 'Why don't you do that, Tony?' he said evenly.

'Good. I will. For starters, I love this lady.' He jerked a thumb as thick as a sausage toward the rear of the limousine. 'What I do for her I do for love, got it?'

Frank's eyes did not leave the mirror. 'Got it, Tony.'

'You see, I'm not some hired fuckin' gun who is out to make her life miserable.'

'Uh-huh.' A black car, a four-wheel drive, a Toyota, had pulled out of a side street and was trailing along behind the Cadillac. Just far back enough to prevent Frank getting a look at the driver.

'I do things the way she likes,' Tony continued, his voice rising slightly. 'Her happiness is everything to me.'

'That's good, Tony.'

'And I think things should be handled the way she likes them to be handled. I know how to do that. You don't. You're nothing but an outsider.'

The Toyota was caught in the mirror as if in a gun sight. Farmer's brain was working in overdrive. Was this a coincidence, a peaceable citizen who just happened to own a vehicle that just happened to be very popular? Was he driving cautiously, keeping his distance, just as the California Highway Patrol suggested? Or was this him, an assassin, playing a nerve-racking game of chicken?

'Are you listening to me, Farmer?'

'Uh-huh. No problem. I'd like to know how you handle things, Tony.'

Tony was surprised by this sudden capitulation. He nodded, slightly mollified. 'That's good. I handle things fine, Frank. You watch me and maybe you'll learn something.'

'Turn left,' Frank ordered curtly.

Henry's eyes flicked into the rear-view mirror, spotting the Toyota instantly. 'Is that him?'

Frank shook his head. 'I'm not sure. Could be.'

'Who? Who him? Who?' Tony tried to turn to look,

but his thick neck couldn't swivel through much more than twenty degrees. He hauled himself bodily around in the seat. 'Hey? What the hell is going on here?'

'Shortcut,' said Frank.

The Cadillac made a smooth left-hand turn, the Toyota following, still tailing at a discreet distance. Both cars were approaching Waverly Lane.

'Henry, slow down. Very slow.'

The chauffeur was anxious to employ his newly learned driving skills. 'You want me to do a one-eighty?' he asked eagerly.

'No. Just slow down.'

Henry touched the power brakes and the big car slowed. Spector and Rachel, deep in conversation in the back seat, looked up.

'Why are we stopping?' Sy Spector demanded.

The Cadillac sat in the middle of the quiet road. The black Toyota stopped too, perfectly framed in the wide rear window of the limousine. If the Toyota was being driven by an ordinary motorist, he would honk his horn or floor the gas pedal to pull past the Caddy. But neither happened.

Make your move, thought Frank. He wanted it to happen now. *Get it over with.*

Instead, as if sensing the challenge in Farmer's gaze, the Toyota's engine suddenly gunned and the driver pulled the vehicle into a tight, tire-screeching left turn, disappearing down a canyon road.

'Let's go,' said Frank.

The instant the limousine stopped at the gates of Rachel Marron's estate, Frank leapt out. 'Take them up to the house,' he ordered.

Then he started running across the expansive lawn of the house, pounding across the grass, headed for the next-door property.

They all stared, watching him disappear into the underbrush of the hillside.

Tony spoke for them all. 'What's with him?'

Frank carried a mental map of the neighborhood running parallel to the road the Toyota had taken. If he was fast enough – and if luck was on his side – he might be able to intersect with the Toyota as it drove down from the hills. He didn't think he would be able to stop the vehicle, but he might get close enough to get a look at the driver or glimpse the license plates. He was sure of one thing – maybe: the driver of the Toyota did not expect Frank Farmer to be chasing him on foot.

He crashed through a couple of expensive gardens on some very secluded property before breaking out on to the steep hillside. His leather-soled dress shoes were not the best footwear for this kind of work, and he skidded down through the grass, unable to get a heel into the dry soil to break his slide.

A retaining wall had been built up from the side of the road to hold back the hillside – the heights around Los Angeles were notoriously unstable during rains and earthquakes. From the top of the wall to the roadside there was a sheer drop of sixteen feet to the asphalt and Frank was slithering toward it a little too fast for comfort.

He managed to brake himself on the narrow concrete lip at the top of the wall, getting back in control of himself. Once steadied, Frank dropped over the side of the wall, plummeting toward the road. The Toyota roared by.

Frank hit the ground hard, allowing his knees to

take some of the impact like shock absorbers. He rolled once in the dust and then sprang up, in a half crouch, as if he expected a gun shot or two.

But the 4 × 4 had pulled around a corner. Far off, Farmer could hear the driver going through the gears as the Toyota zoomed down to the canyon floor.

He slapped the dust off his knees and then began the long, hot walk back up the hillside to the Marron estate.

It took a quick three minutes for Frank to get down the hill, but it required a long, foot-slogging fifteen for him to get back up.

Workmen were hanging the new gate, and the finishing touches were being put on the guard house just inside the beginning of the driveway. Waiting behind the gate, like a welcoming committee, were Henry and Fletcher.

'Did you catch 'em?' asked Fletcher.

'Nope.'

'Next time, Frank,' said Henry with a smile.

'I hope so.' They followed him up the driveway to the house. The Cadillac was sitting in front of the house, the engine ticking and clicking as it cooled.

Frank opened the trunk and took out an attaché case. 'C'mon,' he said. 'I want to show you something.'

'What?' asked Fletcher.

'You'll see.'

Frank led them around the house and they settled at a table on the patio. Down at the pool, Rachel Marron lazed in a chaise, soaking up the sun, wearing a one-piece bathing suit. Through the jet-black lenses of her sunglasses she watched the two men and her son. She sighed and tried to relax. From all over the grounds and from inside the house came the sounds of busy workmen hammering and pounding, building in all the security devices Frank Farmer had ordered – about which she had not been consulted.

Frank Farmer unsnapped the clasps of the attaché case and swung open the top of the valise. Henry and Fletcher peered in. They saw what appeared to be two Walkman-type portable stereos.

Both Henry and Fletcher knew that, with Frank Farmer around, nothing could be that simple.

'These are Surv-Kit communication systems,' said Frank. He took off his suit jacket and clipped the transmitter/receiver on to his belt, resting it in the small of his back. Then he carefully threaded the microphone cord along the right arm of his coat and clipped the tiny voice piece on to the sleeve next to the buttons on his wrist. The other cord, the one with a minute speaker on one end, fitted neatly in his ear. Then he put on his coat.

'You've seen the Secret Service,' he said to Fletcher. 'The guys who protect the President. Well, this is how they keep in contact.'

'Wow,' said Fletcher.

Henry took his device and installed it in his suit jacket, just as Frank Farmer had done.

'We're on the same frequency, Henry. If you want to talk to me, just raise your arm, put your hand to your mouth' – Farmer did so as he spoke – 'and talk into your sleeve.'

Henry laughed when he heard Frank's voice in his earpiece. 'Whoa! I'm receiving you loud and clear.'

'That's the idea.'

Fletcher grabbed Frank's hand and spoke into the fake wrist button. 'Tell me about the car.'

Farmer smiled down at the little boy. 'Toyota. Black.'

'Four-wheel drive? What model? Is it new? Or is it old and beat up?'

'New.'

'A C5 V6 Toyota Four-Runner, right?'

'That's right, Fletcher.'

'I knew it!'

'One problem, though. One little snag.'

Fletcher's smile vanished. 'What?'

'There are 360,000 vehicles answering that description in greater Los Angeles. Probably a couple of million of them in the whole country.'

'How do you know?'

'I checked. But you did good, noticing all that.'

Fletcher shrugged. 'Well,' he said philosophically, 'nobody is perfect, right, Frank?'

'That's right.'

Rachel Marron's eyes kept on straying back to Farmer and Fletcher on the patio. The scene annoyed her. Her little boy was plainly very taken with the bodyguard, and somehow that got under her skin. Fletcher was too sophisticated for obvious hero worship, but she could see that he looked up to Farmer, admired him in a way that only a boy can admire a no-nonsense man of action. It was a role she could never fill, no matter how big a star, no matter the number of Oscars and Grammies.

She shifted on the chaise, as if she could not get comfortable on the soft pool bed. The whining of a powerful drill boring into metal shrieked out of the house. The jagged sound seemed to be aimed straight at her ear, piercing her brain. She jumped to her feet.

'Shut up, you assholes!' she yelled at the house. There was no appreciable reduction in noise.

Fletcher looked down at his mother. 'Uh-oh. Mom's on the war path. I'm outta here.'

'Me too,' said Henry.

'You know,' said Frank, 'I think we should go check out the new surveillance cameras.'

'Good idea.'

The two men and the child stole into the house, like naughty boys escaping the stern eye of a cranky old teacher.

The whole house and the grounds were alive with noise and workmen. Somewhere a cement mixer went around and around, making a rasping, grinding sound that was really getting on her nerves. From time to time the technicians installing the alarms in the house tested their handiwork, the sirens blasting out over the usually peaceful gardens.

Irritated, Rachel slipped on her Walkman, pumped up the volume and lay back in the sunlight. Her own voice filled her ears, but her new song couldn't keep out the shriek of the alarms and the puncturing wail of drills and the hammer of power tools.

She stripped off the headphones and stared angrily at her home, as if all of this noise was the fault of the building itself.

'Okay,' she growled. 'Enough!' Abruptly she sat up and swung her legs off the couch.

She was going to go up to the house, lock herself in her bedroom, turn up her stereo and her air conditioning as high as they would go and try to forget that her peaceful home had been invaded.

She encountered Nicki on the patio. 'Call Charlie's,' Rachel instructed her sister. 'Tell Arlene we'll be six for brunch tomorrow instead of the usual.' Charlie's was a restaurant out at the beach where Rachel was a valued, regular customer. She knew all the employees by name and they loved her for it.

Nicki grimaced. 'Um . . . Rachel? Farmer says that we shouldn't go to Charlie's tomorrow.'

Rachel's face darkened. 'We'll see about that! Call Devaney. Get him up here. Now!'

'Yes, Rachel. I'll get right on it.'

Rachel stormed into the house, quickly climbed the stairs to the second floor and pushed open the door of her bedroom, stripping off her bathing suit the instant she crossed the threshold.

Then she stopped in the middle of the room, naked, and stared bug-eyed at the elderly locksmith who was fiddling with the catch on the tall bedroom windows. He stared back, his mouth agape, awestruck.

Rachel was so angry that she looked like a boiler about to blow. She clutched the bathing suit to her breasts, trying to hide herself behind a skimpy handful of filmy material. It was the last straw.

'You! You! Out! Out! Now!' she screamed. This time Rachel's voice could be heard all over the house, above the din made by the workmen.

The locksmith, terrified, dropped his tools and started backing toward the door. He walked cautiously, as if Rachel were a wild animal and a sudden movement would spook her into attacking him, tooth and claw.

'Out of here! Get out!'

'Yes, ma'am,' he stammered. Despite the terrifying situation he found himself in, he couldn't stop himself from running an approving eye over Rachel's svelte body, as if trying to memorize every detail and curve.

'I said *out*!'

'Yes, ma'am. Thank you, ma'am. I'm going.'

'And take your tools with you!'

The man bent and grabbed his tool box and raced for the door. 'I'm a real big fan of yours, Miss Marron.'

Rachel didn't care – she was not in the habit of entertaining fans in her bedroom. She slammed the door behind the old workman and then threw herself on the bed, pummeling the mattress and screaming into the pillows.

The telephone next to her bed buzzed quietly. Rachel grabbed the receiver.

'What?' she snapped.

'Bill Devaney is here, Rachel,' said Nicki softly.

'Good!' she snarled. She dressed quickly, then charged across the house to find most of her support team assembled in the family room. Sy Spector was perched uneasily on the edge of a bar stool. Devaney paced nervously. Rory, the choreographer, leaned on the counter where Nicki stood methodically chopping fruit and dropping it into a shiny silver blender.

'Rachel, honey,' said Rory, 'you look tense.'

'I *am* tense,' she snapped. 'Who wouldn't be?'

'Come here, darling. I'll rub your back.' Rory stood behind her and began kneading and massaging her neck and shoulders. Rachel squirmed under his firm fingers. 'Oooh, you are tight, honey. You have to relax.'

'I'll relax when he's gone,' she said sharply. There was no need to say who 'he' was.

Devaney sighed. Getting Frank Farmer had been hard enough. Keeping him looked like it might be impossible. 'What is it now, Rachel?'

'He told Rachel no Sunday brunch at Charlie's,' Nicki explained quickly. She neatly peeled a peach, quartered it and dropped it into the blender.

Devaney's shoulders sagged, as if a great weight had been laid upon them. 'No Sunday brunch?' Rachel Marron's personal manager shook his head. 'No Sunday brunch? That's why you called me up here?'

'It's not just that,' Rachel replied angrily. 'It's my money and it's my life and I want him out of here.'

'Where is he?' Devaney asked wearily.

'On the patio,' said Nicki.

Devaney walked to the french doors and opened them.

'He's through messing with my life,' Rachel said firmly. 'Are you getting this, Bill?'

Devaney turned angrily. 'Rachel, I'm getting goddamn sick of running up here every time he steps on your toes.'

'You'll come running up here when I tell you to,' Rachel shot back. 'Don't you forget you work for me!'

The room was very still and her angry, contemptuous words seemed to hang in the air like acrid smoke. Sy Spector, Rory and Nicki looked around the room, unwilling to rest their eyes on the combatants. They felt like outsiders, intruders in a vicious family argument. Nicki busied herself with skinning and chopping a pineapple. Without looking up she dumped the pulp in the blender, then added a dollop of yogurt.

Devaney and Rachel locked in an angry stare. For a moment it looked as if he was going to take up the gauntlet that his tempestuous star had hurled at his feet. Devaney had a choice: he could escalate the argument – and the only weapon he had was the threat of resignation, and Rachel, in her present mood, just might accept it – or he could save his job and his fortune and back down.

The man hesitated a moment, as if trying to make up his mind. Then he ground his teeth and leaned out of the doorway. 'Farmer! Would you come in here a minute?'

Rachel realized that she had pushed too hard and tried to defuse the tension. 'Did you *know* he was nuts,

Bill?' She managed a little smile, as if Farmer's actions were no fault of her manager.

'Do you know who couldn't get past the gates this morning?' asked Spector.

'Who?'

'Robin Leach, that's who!' To a publicist, the diminutive, balding, buzz-saw-voiced host of *Lifestyles of the Rich and Famous* and noted television spokesman for an auto parts company, had a mystical, semi-divine status.

Unfortunately for Spector, the others in the room did not esteem the gossipmonger quite as much as Sy did. Rory stifled a giggle, sniggering into Rachel's hair, fighting off a laugh. His snickers set off a chain reaction. Rachel and Nicki both had trouble keeping a straight face.

'You think that's funny?' said Sy Spector sourly. 'The man talks to twenty million people a week and he can't even get in here.'

'Did he have an appointment?' Frank Farmer stood framed in the doorway.

'Robin Leach doesn't need an appointment!'

'From now on he does. That goes for everybody.' Farmer glanced from face to face, as if daring them to contradict him.

Spector was irate. 'Farmer, the quickest way to get killed in this town is to alienate the press.' The publicist immediately regretted his choice of words. He tried to dismiss what he had just said with an offhand wave. 'Anyway, you know what I mean,' he mumbled.

'Never mind that,' said Devaney. 'Farmer, what is this about brunch at Charlie's? Rachel has been going to Charlie's every Sunday for the last five years.'

'I don't want her doing anything she's always done.'

Rachel pitched her voice low and spoke slowly,

mimicking her bodyguard. ' "I don't want her doing anything she's always done." The guy is a fanatic,' she said to no one in particular, like a doctor diagnosing a disease.

'So are the guys he's protecting you from,' said Devaney quietly.

Rachel shot him a withering, contemptuous glance. 'Excuse me if I don't faint.'

'Rachel, think of Fletcher –' The rest of Nicki's words were drowned out when, disdainfully, Rachel switched on the blender. The blades of the machine whirred, whipping up the fruit. Frank stared coolly at Rachel, secretly amazed that she would humiliate her sister in front of her friends and colleagues. Rachel met his stare, gazing at him petulantly, defiantly. She turned off the blender and the appliance ground to a stop.

She took the top off the blender bowl and examined the contents. 'Do you know he's got the phones bugged?'

'Oh, Jesus, Bill,' said Spector. 'That's going too far.' The publicist colored slightly, thinking of some of the calls he had made from the Marron house – calls he would just as soon keep private.

'Maybe he gets off listening to my calls.' Her voice was taunting, derisive, and she spoke as if Frank Farmer was not in the room. 'You know, all that heavy breathing . . .'

'Rachel,' said Devaney angrily, 'just what the hell do you want from me? What do you want from *my* life?'

'I want some peace around here,' she snapped. 'All this noise! The strangers . . .'

'That's right,' said Spector. He took care always to be on the same side of an issue as his star.

Devaney looked to Farmer imploringly. 'Frank? Can you arrange some peace around here?'

It occurred to Farmer that Rachel didn't seem to mind noise and confusion and invasions of strangers when she had her house redecorated, but he let it pass. 'We're almost done,' he said.

'And I want to be able to eat brunch with my friends,' said Rachel, like a demanding, spoiled child.

'You can eat brunch. Just go on Tuesday this week.'

Spector looked at Frank as if he were an alien who had just landed in Rachel Marron's family room. Sunday brunch was an institution in Hollywood. Tuesday brunch was unheard of.

'Tuesday morning brunch?' The publicist shook his head in wonderment and then looked at Devaney. 'Where the hell did you find this guy?'

CHAPTER EIGHT

Rachel Marron loved to shop and, as befitted her wealth, her shopping sprees were usually centered on the chic, expensive shops of Beverly Hills and Santa Monica. Merchants up and down Rodeo Drive and on Main Street loved to see Rachel's limousine pull up in front of their shops – rare was the day when Rachel hit the stores that she didn't spend somewhere in the five figures.

But there was another side to her shopping. Once in a while she went downscale, heading for West Los Angeles and a thrift shop on Veteran Avenue in Palms. It wasn't a slum exactly, but the neighborhood was definitely a little down at the heel – not an area where you'd expect to encounter a giant Cadillac limo like Rachel's.

The car cruised up to the curb in front of Louise's, a second-hand clothing store where she always found something eccentric or funky to add to her already enormous wardrobe.

Frank, in the back seat with Rachel, looked at the slightly disreputable street and the run-down shop front and shook his head. Why was his charge determined to put herself in danger?

Rachel caught his look of disapproval. 'Don't take it personally, Farmer,' she said, climbing out of the car. 'I came here before you showed up and I'll still be coming here when you are long gone.'

He leaned forward and tapped Tony on the shoulder. 'Watch the car. And keep your eye on them.' Farmer pointed to a knot of teenagers standing around on the sidewalk on the far side of the street. They were eyeing the car enviously.

'What about me?' asked Henry.

'Watch Tony.'

'I wish Rachel didn't keep coming here,' Henry said. 'It makes me nervous.'

'Me too,' said Tony with a grin. ''Cept I'm not nervous 'cos I got *you* with me.'

Frank followed his employer into the shabby store. There were racks of second-hand clothes everywhere, and Rachel had fallen on them enthusiastically, riffling through the hangers as if she was shuffling cards. Frank's eyes scanned the room and he pulled back the curtain that separated the makeshift changing cubicle from the rest of the store. He was relieved to see that there was no one else in the shop besides Louise, the proprietor.

'Louise!' exclaimed Rachel. 'You've got too much great stuff here!'

Louise was in the back of the store. She knew from experience that it was better to leave Rachel alone – she bought more that way. The owner laughed loudly. 'Well, it's all for sale. Take it all, darlin'.'

Frank leaned against a wall, strategically placed near the door, his eyes darting, glancing out into the street every few seconds.

Rachel pulled a dress off one of the racks and held it out in front of her. 'Woooo! Let me try this one on.' She glanced over at Frank and felt a twinge of disappointment. He was still watching the street – a sight he seemed to find more interesting than her.

She swept back the curtain of the changing booth, then paused dramatically. 'Farmer, do you want to come in here with me? You know, just to be on the safe side?'

Frank looked at her for a second, then, without a word, resumed his surveillance.

Rachel stepped into the changing room and peered over the low wall. 'You probably won't believe this, Farmer, but I have a reputation for being a bitch.'

Frank's eyes never left the street. Some of the kids on the sidewalk had come over to the limo and were talking to Tony and Henry. It was nothing to worry about, nothing more than harmless street play – they were horsing around, exchanging good-natured insults with the two men or gawking at the plush interior of the car. Their jokes and laughter crackled in Frank's ear, picked up by Henry's Surv-Kit and relayed to Frank's receiver. It seemed that Tony's considerable bulk had dispelled any ideas they may have had of causing trouble.

'Farmer? Are you listening to me?'

Frank nodded.

'Good.' She was zipping up the back of her dress. 'I didn't use to be – a bitch, I mean. But you know how it is. You get known for being a certain way – the way people think you are – and pretty soon you get like that.' She shrugged, as if settling the dress on her shoulders and excusing her behavior at the same time. 'Can't help it.'

Frank smiled knowingly, a little facial expression that seemed to contradict everything she had said.

'Oh, you don't think so? You're such an expert on famous people?'

'I've seen a few.'

'And you disagree? You don't think you become what the public wants? That's how it is,' she said with an air of finality.

Frank's voice was flat, matter-of-fact. 'You can be as you choose to be. It's an act of discipline sometimes, but it can be done.'

Rachel swept aside the curtain of the changing room and stepped in front of the mirror. She spoke to Frank's reflection in the glass.

'That's why you never stay with your clients? They too undisciplined for you? Or is it you're afraid you'll start to care about them?'

Frank wasn't much interested in her amateur attempts at psychoanalysis. 'Yeah, that's right,' he said dismissively.

Rachel turned angrily. 'Can't you answer straight, just once? Why don't you talk to me? I'm not such a bad lady.'

'Oh, you're too clever for me. I can't keep up.' He continued his vigilant examination of the street.

Rachel stepped up close to him. He could smell her perfume and sense the anger that tremored through her. 'Look at me, Farmer!'

Reluctantly, he tore his eyes from the window and looked at her inquiringly.

'You don't approve of me, do you?'

'Disapproval is a luxury I can't afford,' he said smoothly. 'Gets in the way.'

'Don't like emotions getting to you, huh?' Her voice was mocking, scornful. And yet it seemed to Farmer that she was coming on to him, flirting with him behind her anger. 'Never mix business with pleasure, right?'

Frank nodded. 'That's right.' If she expected him to open up to her, then she was to be disappointed. It was a stand-off – he was not willing to give an inch and she was not prepared to go any further. Like a spring extended to its greatest length, she snapped back, recoiling into her guise of movie star and Frank's employer.

'Get me that dress,' she said, pointing at the first one on the rack that her eyes fell upon.

Frank stood stock-still for a moment, then resumed his inspection of the street scene outside. 'I'm here to keep you alive,' he said quietly, 'not to help you shop.'

'Dammit!' She snatched up the dress and whipped the changing-booth curtain closed.

Frank smiled.

Rachel Marron hardly ever spent a quiet night at home. Her nocturnal hours were a cycle of dinners, parties and premières, a social round that seemed never-ending. It was not the way Frank would have chosen to do things – every time Rachel left the compound she was in danger – but even he realized that part and parcel of being a star was being seen. She had to be seen, not just by her adoring public but by other stars, by people in the industry, by the press. Business and pleasure were indistinguishable.

Nicki had informed Frank that dinner that night was an entourage-only affair at Morton's – it was Monday after all. He anticipated no problems. There might be a few gawkers on the sidewalk, hoping to catch a glimpse of Morton's hip and powerful clientele, but within the restaurant itself the calm cool of the very famous would prevail. The kitchen help and waiters at some Los Angeles restaurants were sometimes secretly on the payroll of gossip magazines, tabloid newspapers and paparazzi and they would tip off their employers when a particularly big star showed up. This was not tolerated at Morton's.

'Casual dinner,' Nicki had told him. 'Blue jeans. Rachel says nothing fancy.' Farmer had laughed when he heard that: a nothing-fancy, blue-jeans-only dinner in a restaurant where the cheapest wine on the wine list was seventy-five dollars. Still, he was relieved. Rachel would encounter no trouble at Morton's.

Frank w███ ███rried about the car. Morton's had an a███ ███round parking garage, and no one ███ ███tay with the car once it had d███ ███ncrete cave. It would be a sim███ ███e unauthorized to gain access t███ ███with what the Secret Service ███ an 'explosive device', as 'bomb'

███ ███he car around to the front of the ███nk was waiting. He opened the trunk ███ and removed a long, light aluminum po███ ██at an angle about two-thirds of the way down t██ shaft. At the very tip was a wide mirror.

'Come here, Henry,' said Frank, 'I want you to see this.'

'What is that thing?'

Farmer slid the mirror end of the pole beneath the Cadillac, the mirror reflecting the muddy machinery that made up the undercarriage of the long vehicle.

'What the hell are you doing? Checking for rust?' the young man asked with a grin.

'No.' Farmer was slowly walking the length of the car, his eyes fixed on the mirror. 'I'm checking for bombs.'

'Bombs! I have met the only bomb I ever want to meet,' Henry said, holding up his still bandaged hand. 'You know, Farmer, I think I'm going to get into a safer line of work. Something nice and restful. Like boxing.'

Frank laughed. 'I know what you mean.'

'Have you ever been blown up?'

'No,' admitted Frank. 'People have tried to stab me. I've been shot at, punched, kicked and black-jacked. But I have never had the distinction of being blown up.'

'Then you *don't* know what I mean,' said Henry with a laugh. 'There is nothing else like it.'

People were coming out of the house, first Devaney and Spector, then Rachel Marron. Frank looked at her and scowled.

'What's the matter, Farmer? Don't you like my outfit? I didn't realize you had an eye for fashion.' Rachel was dressed to the nines in a tight-fitting, short, slinky black dress and high heels. Either Rachel had broken her own dress code or they weren't going to nice, safe, discreet Morton's.

'I thought it was dinner, Henry. A quiet dinner at Morton's.'

Henry shrugged. 'I thought you knew. Change of plan.'

'We're going somewhere else? Where are we going?'

Spector waved a video tape at him. 'The Mayan, Frank. We're going to the Mayan.'

'What's the Mayan?'

Spector started to climb into the limousine. 'It's a club, Frank. C'mon, Henry, let's go.'

Frank Farmer grabbed Sy Spector by the upper arm, preventing him from getting into the car. 'A club? What kind of club, Spector? Is it a private club?'

'No, it's a music club. A dance club.' Then, as if translating something into a foreign language. 'You'd probably call it a disco.'

'Spector,' said Frank angrily, 'you have got to tell me about these things.'

'I just did.' He settled in the back seat next to Bill Devaney. He leaned foward and called out through the open door. 'C'mon, Rachel. We'll be late.'

Rachel was at the door, saying goodbye to Fletcher.

The little boy was standing in the hallway dwarfed by the two uniformed security guards standing on either side of him.

''Bye, honey,' she said, kneeling down to give him a little peck on the cheek. 'I don't want you still to be up when I get home.'

'I won't be.'

'Promise?'

'Promise, Mom.'

'Good.' She turned to find Frank standing directly behind her.

Fletcher smiled and waved. ''Bye, Frank.'

'So long, pal.'

He escorted Rachel to the waiting automobile. 'What's the matter?' she asked. 'You think I'm going to get rubbed out on my own doorstep.'

'No.'

She changed tack, tugging at his lapels and pretending to brush some lint off his shoulders. 'Nice suit, Frank,' she said disdainfully.

The cheap cop in a cheap suit was a cliché Frank didn't much care for. 'Miss Marron.'

'What?'

He pulled a small red leather box from his pocket, a jewel box, as if he was about to propose. 'I want you to have this.'

'What is it?'

'Open it.' Both of them were aware that Spector and Devaney were watching them closely. Sy had popped open a bottle of champagne and the two men were sitting and sipping, watching the bodyguard and his employer as if they were actors in a play.

Rachel prised open the case. Lying on a little bed of velvet was a red, green and gold enamel cross a little bigger than a pendant. Rachel gazed at it a moment, flattered and confused. This was the last thing she would have expected from Frank Farmer.

'This is for me?' she stammered. 'It's beautiful.'

Frank lifted the cross from the case and turned it over, showing her the clasp on the back. 'It's fitted with a transmitter,' he said. 'When you close the clasp, it sends a signal.' He tapped his earpiece. 'If there's ever a problem and we're separated, just press it and I'll know you need me.'

Rachel was flustered and wasn't quite sure how to respond, stuck for words. It was a strange little speech. On one hand it was Frank Farmer, bodyguard, giving the woman under his care instructions on how to contact him in the case of an emergency. On the other, his language was curiously like that of a lover.

For a moment, their eyes locked. Then Sy Spector broke the magic moment. 'Okay,' he barked, 'she knows how it works. Let's get going.'

Rachel managed to flash Frank a dazzling smile before disappearing into the back of the car.

Frank eased himself into the front seat next to Tony. The big man turned on the radio and settled in his seat.

'Tell me about the Mayan, Tony.'

He shrugged. 'It's a club. Very big. What's to tell? It's popular.'

'Great,' said Frank hollowly. He could guess what the Mayan was like: dark, crowded, possibly a death trap. The only thing going for him was that, if going to the Mayan was a last-minute plan with Rachel, chances were good that no one else knew about it. His moment of relief, grasping at that particular straw, did not last long.

Just as Henry made the turn, guiding the big car on to Doheny, the disc jockey on the radio broke in to the music. 'It's the top of the hour and you're listening to KROK, LA's premier rock station and, yes, we have news. We told you we'd crack the case of the mystery guest – and we have. If you are one of the few who haven't heard by now, tonight's secret performer at the Mayan is – drum roll, please – Rachel!'

Frank jumped as if he had been stung. 'Rachel?'

'And, of course, I mean Rachel,' continued the DJ, 'as in the Queen of the Night, the "I Have Nothing" poster girl herself: Rachel Marron.'

Everyone in the car was sitting still, frozen, their champagne glasses half-way to their mouths, listening to the words spilling out of the speakers.

'What the hell is going on?' demanded Farmer.

The disc jockey's patter continued. 'Rachel Marron, tonight appearing as Billy Thomas's very special guest. Word is, Rachel is going to debut some hot new material tonight. But if you don't have a ticket, you can forget going down there. We just got word that the place is packed. Yes, the KROK spies are everywhere.'

Frank was slumped in his seat, shaking his head. 'Son of a bitch,' he muttered. Was she *trying* to get killed?

Suddenly the atmosphere in the limousine was tense, nervousness pervading the air. Devaney looked as worried as the bodyguard, and Rachel's eyes were wide with anxiety. Sy Spector looked guilty.

'How did they find out, Sy?' Devaney was tight-lipped, his eyes narrowing suspiciously.

'It wasn't me.'

Frank Farmer turned around in the seat. 'Was this your idea of good publicity, Spector? Just couldn't resist, could you? Damn.' He turned back in his seat and stared fixedly forward.

'Watch your mouth, Farmer. I don't have to take that kind of shit from you.' Then he turned to Rachel. 'It really wasn't me. Honest. You have to believe me.'

'*Sure*, Sy, I believe you.'

'This is a public service announcement from KROK,' said the DJ, ''cause the police have asked us to ask you to stay away. So, everybody, please stay cool, stay tuned, and we'll try to get you some interviews after the show. Remember, you heard it here on KROK – K-Rock, LA, the station that delivers.'

They were approaching the Mayan now, and Frank blanched when he saw the huge crowd, hundreds of people packed on to the narrow sidewalk, spilling into the street.

It was Frank's worse nightmare, but Tony, staring at the mob, put it in words: 'Fuckin' A,' he said. 'This looks like trouble.'

CHAPTER NINE

Almost everyone in the limousine was unhappy about the crowd waiting for Rachel outside the Mayan. Frank was unhappy for obvious reasons. Rachel was gloomy because she wanted to try out her new material with a few unsuspecting clubgoers, not die-hard fans; she wanted genuine feedback, not blind adoration. Devaney was unhappy because all he wanted was a nice peaceful life – and a star performer alive and kicking. In a mass of humanity like this there was no guarantee he would get either.

The lone exception was Sy Spector. A capacity crowd, unruly now and bound for frenzy later, would garner acres of newspaper coverage plus a mention on the local TV news; he was sure he would get *Entertainment Tonight* and CNN, as well as wrap-around reporting on E! Entertainment Network. And maybe they were angry at him now, but who could blame a man for doing his job? Actually, it hadn't been his idea to leak Rachel's appearance at the Mayan, but that was his little secret . . .

The mob on the sidewalk let out a roar as the limousine approached. There was no sound quite like the clamor of a swarm like that. They were Rachel Marron fans, but they sounded menacing, low-voiced and threatening – a multitude of crazed followers, teetering on the fine line between love and hate. No one could predict on which side of the line they would fall.

The people streamed off the pavement and surrounded the car, pounding on the roof and peering in the window. There was a barrage of blinding flash-bulbs and the steady stream of hot white light from the flood beam of a television video camera. Security guards were on the scene, trying to clear a path for Rachel's car, but you didn't have to be an expert to see that they were over-reacting. A man had been clubbed and he stumbled against the car, the blood from his nose splattering the tinted window.

Frank could see Henry out of the corner of his eye. He was hesitating, ready to slam on the brakes if the crowd got in front of the car.

'Don't stop,' said Frank calmly. 'Don't slow down. Just keep moving. They don't love her enough to get run over.' *And the hell with them if they do*, he added as a silent afterthought. He immediately moved to calm himself down. The situation required a level head, not anger.

The guards managed to hold the crowd back long enough for Henry to make the right-hand turn into the secured parking lot next door to the Mayan.

'I suggest calling it off. Now,' said Frank.

'Don't be ridiculous,' snapped Sy Spector.

'Frank,' pleaded Devaney, 'they'll tear the place apart. Look at them, for Christ's sake!'

'They'll tear it apart anyway,' said Frank. His voice was unruffled, composed. 'We just won't be here when it happens.'

'No,' said Rachel firmly. 'They won't do anything as long as I give them a show.'

'Okay,' said Frank. 'You're the boss.' He jumped out of the car and opened the door. Rachel stepped out and immediately underwent a profound change. A moment before, she had been annoyed, even scared, but now she was all performer. She pasted a wide, delighted show-biz smile on her face – her public face – and waved to her fans.

They were pushing against the cordon of security guards, yelling, screaming, waving. Some people were crying. A chant went up: 'Rachel! Rachel! We want Rachel!'

She was sandwiched between Spector and Devaney, Tony in front of her, Frank bringing up the rear. A young man broke through the cordon of security guards and raced for Rachel.

Restrained, almost gentle, Frank caught the fellow long before he reached the star and guided him back to the line of guards. One of them raised his truncheon, ready to club the interloper.

'No need for that,' said Frank. 'No harm done.' He hurried to catch up with Rachel and her followers, joining them at the stage door.

She knew her way around backstage at the Mayan and headed directly for the large dressing room set aside for stars. Frank got to the door before her and stepped in, running a practised eye over the room.

There was no one waiting there for her but there were huge bouquets of flowers everywhere, giant and elaborate arrangements filling the room. Frank pulled a device from his pocket that looked like a TV remote control with a short hoop of thick silver wire attached.

He turned on the contraption and ran the ring over the flowers.

Rachel snorted and rolled her eyes. 'What the hell is that thing?'

'Magnometer.'

'What you looking for? Bombs?'

'That's right.'

'I *don't* think anyone is going to blow me up.'

For a moment Frank stopped, then continued his

examination of the flowers. They still hadn't told her about the booby-trapped doll . . .

'Well,' he said after a moment. 'Better safe than sorry.'

'Yeah, yeah.' Rachel sat down at the dressing table and turned on the stage lights that surrounded the big mirror. She examined her make-up, took out a lipstick and touched up her lips.

'Well, I'll say this for you, Farmer, you are thorough.'

'That's what you pay me for.'

The flower arrangement closest to the dressing table was an exquisite spray of lilies of the valley. It was not the largest or most ornate or even most expensive array in the room, but it was the loveliest. The envelope that accompanied it was marked, simply, 'Rachel.' She plucked the note from the arrangement and opened it.

Then she screamed.

Frank whipped around, throwing away the magnometer, one hand going for his gun, the other reaching for Rachel to pull her to the floor. He stopped when he saw her face in the mirror, shocked and petrified.

At the sound of the door opening, he turned again. This time the gun was in his hand.

Devaney threw his hands up, as if they would protect him from a 9-millimeter bullet. Spector was right behind him.

'Jesus Christ, Farmer!'

'Shut the door.'

'We heard a scream. Did she scream?' demanded Spector.

'Rachel? Are you okay.'

Rachel Marron had not moved. She was seated at the mirror, trembling, dazed. She still held the card in her hand. Frank holstered his gun and took the note.

Tiny letters had been cut from a book, a dictionary perhaps, characters small enough to fit on the diminutive note card. The message, though, was strong – and familiar. 'marron bitch – you have everything. i have nothing – prepare your soul for death – the time to die is coming.'

Frank Farmer passed the note to Devaney.

'Oh, my God,' he breathed. 'He sent another one.'

Rachel seemed to come out of her trance with a snap. 'What do you mean "another one"?'

Frank shot a glance at Spector. 'They didn't tell you?'

Rachel looked bewildered. 'Tell me? Tell me what?'

Devaney cleared his throat and shuffled his feet, scuffing them against the carpet. 'There were some other letters before, Rachel. The same sort of thing, threats, you know, oddball stuff . . .'

'We didn't want to worry you,' said Spector soothingly. 'We thought we'd take care of it.'

'See, someone got into the house . . .'

Rachel suddenly felt sick to her stomach, her gorge rising. She struggled to fight the nausea and the panic that were building up inside her. 'Someone was in my house?'

'Okay,' said Spector, as if calming a child frightened of thunder, 'let's not get hysterical . . .'

'Let's get her out of here,' said Frank firmly.

Rachel ignored him, still trying to take in what she had just been told. 'Someone was in my *house*?'

'It was weeks ago,' said Spector. 'You were out of town. We didn't want to worry you with it. We're here to deal with things like that.'

'No,' said Farmer. 'I'm here to deal with things like that and I say she can't –'

'Fletcher,' gasped Rachel. 'Was it while Fletcher was there?'

'Hey, c'mon. Fletcher is okay. The house is like Fort Knox now. Right, Frank?'

'We should get her out of here. Right now!'

'Frank, don't over-react!' Spector could see his publicity coup going up in smoke. 'There's no way anyone could . . . I mean, no one would be crazy enough to . . .'

'There's no way anyone could what?' Rachel was scared now, and her shaky voice betrayed her fear.

'No, wait. Look, everybody, calm down. Just calm down.' Sy lowered his voice, as if trying to quiet a spooked horse.

'Sy,' said Devaney. 'Frank's right.'

'Let's ask Rachel,' said Spector, as if he had just had a brilliant idea. 'We'll put it to her. How do you feel, honey?'

Frank folded his arms across his chest. His anger was building as fast as Rachel's terror. 'I'll put this as plainly as I can. Maybe it will have some bearing on what we're talking about here. *I cannot protect her out there.* Got it? Is that simple enough?'

Rachel turned to look at Bill Devaney. 'Do you think he's out there?'

Devaney shrugged. 'I don't know.'

She turned to Frank, her features hardening. 'He's here, isn't he?'

Frank nodded. 'He might be.'

'C'mon, guys,' said Spector quickly. 'We don't know that. We really don't know that.'

The question of performing that night faded as a more horrible thought came back to her. 'You knew he was in my house and you didn't tell me . . . I can't believe it . . . Oh, my God.'

Devaney threw up his hands. It was obvious to him that Rachel was in no condition to go on stage. 'Let's go home, Sy. We'll have to make an announcement.'

'Fine,' said Spector. 'You make the announcement. You take the responsibility for them tearing the fuckin' place down to the foundations. Listen.' Even deep backstage they could hear the clamor out in the club. The audience was clapping and shouting, braying for Rachel Marron. 'You want that audience? Be my guest.'

'It's gotta be done, Sy,' said Devaney. 'Sorry.'

'Brave man,' sneered Spector.

When Bill Devaney stepped on to the Mayan's stage a wave of noise swept out of the audience, buffeting him. The crowd was restless, impatient, ready for the show to begin. He walked to the mike in the middle of the stage, wading through the sound as if through a swamp. In a room with a thousand people, he had never felt so alone in his life.

Devaney tapped the mike with his finger and the noise abated only a fraction.

'Excuse me . . .' Feedback shimmered through the air. 'I've got an announcement to make. I'm sorry, but . . . due to circumstances beyond –'

'Where's Rachel?' someone screamed.

'Rachel is, uh, unfortunately –'

They knew what was coming. The cascade of boos surged, drowning out his words. Then, below the cat-calls, the chant began again: 'Rachel! Rachel! Rachel!' They were clapping and stamping their feet, keeping time with their chant. The building seemed to tremble as if rocked by an earthquake.

Frank had almost gotten Rachel to the stage-door exit when the chant began. Then she stopped, the look on her face – fear, humiliation – clearing as if the sun had come out after a storm.

'Wait,' she said. 'You hear that?'

Frank could tell what she was thinking. 'Rachel, don't do it. It's not worth it.'

But the chant, the applause – they were mesmerizing, so hypnotic that she didn't notice that he had, for the first time, called her by her first name.

Frank grasped her by the elbow and tried to guide her through the door, but she shook him off angrily. 'No fucking freak is gonna chase me off stage.'

A thunderous roar greeted Rachel when she walked out into the lights, her public smile on. She stood in the torrent of applause for a moment, letting it wash over her, drinking it in as if she was parched and thirsty for adulation. She bowed and clapped back at her fans and then gestured toward Bill Devaney, urging her audience to give him a hand. A moment before, he had been the enemy, but with a single gesture from Rachel the fans roared and clapped for him.

Rachel stepped up to the mike. 'My manager, ladies and gentlemen, Bill Devaney. Thank you, Bill. I have to say, you are one lousy opening act.' It wasn't the greatest joke, but the audience screamed with laughter. The tension defused. Devaney bowed his way off stage, sweat streaming down his brow.

Rachel turned and faced her public, peering out into the lights. 'Hello!' she called, as if she knew each and every one of them personally. 'Isn't Billy Thomas, the owner of this joint, the greatest? He asked me to sing you a song. Hope you don't mind . . .'

Frank was in the wings, trying to see through the barrier of stage lights, nervously scanning for trouble. From where he stood he could see that Rachel was quivering with fear, but she was fighting it, refusing to give in.

She shot a glance over her shoulder, smiled fleetingly, and as the music came up, alone and vulnerable, bathed in light, center stage, she began to sing 'I Have Nothing'.

CHAPTER TEN

Rachel's voice filled the air. Her audience, so rowdy just a few moments before, sat motionless in their seats, transfixed by the sweet music.

Frank was just a few inches offstage, hidden from view behind the wing curtain, ready to swing into action if necessary. Things were calmer now, but Farmer knew that situations like this could change in a matter of seconds. Rachel had led the crowd into serenity, but there was no guarantee it would stay there.

Just then Frank Farmer's major problem was backstage. Sy Spector sidled up to him, positioning himself between the bodyguard and his view of his client.

'Are we having a communications problem here or what?' Sy Spector asked.

'What are you talking about?' Frank knew that Spector had hit the nail on the head: they did have a communications problem – Frank thought that Spector was communicating altogether too much. He wished they didn't have to communicate at all.

Spector's presence was nothing more than a distraction. Farmer tried to look around the man, stepping to one side for a better view, keeping Rachel directly in his line of sight. Like a schoolyard bully taunting a younger, weaker boy, Spector moved too, deliberately obstructing Frank's view.

'Apparently I didn't make things clear enough,' said Spector through clenched teeth.

Farmer looked over the publicist's shoulder. 'Make what clear, Spector?'

'I didn't make it clear to you how things go around here.'

Frank took his eyes off Rachel for a moment and looked sharply at Spector. 'One thing is clear, Spector – you lied to me. You told me you were going to tell her about the stuff that's been going on. And you didn't. No wonder she's been fighting this. You can't protect someone who doesn't know she needs it.'

'Look, I didn't tell her because I didn't think she could handle it. Okay? That's all it was.'

'But she handled it fine.' Frank's eyes flicked back to the stage. There was something approaching admiration in his glance. Soothed and nurtured by the obvious admiration of her audience, Rachel's fear had vanished and she was beginning to soar.

Spector, seeing that confrontation was not going to help him attain his goals, changed tack, becoming confiding, man-to-man. For a moment he considered putting his arm on Frank's shoulder but decided that Farmer would probably not like that.

'Look, Frank, I know what you're saying – I know what this is all about. I know you want to do what's best for her. I understand that.'

'Then there's no problem,' said Frank.

'Well, Frank, I'm sorry to say that there is. You see, you have a job to do here, but what you have to understand is that you're not the only one. You're not the only one with a job to do.'

'I'm keeping her alive. Anyone have a higher priority than that?'

'No, of course not. No one questions that. But Rachel's job is important. So is mine. Her job is to get out *there*.' He jabbed a finger at the brightly lit stage. 'She's working, Frank. That's what she does and that's where she does it. She's hot right now. This is the time for her. She does the right things now and she'll be a star for life. She screws up and in a year she'll be Rachel Who?'

'But she'll be alive,' countered Farmer.

'If she doesn't get out there, *then* she's dead. Forget about the crazy death threats. If she doesn't sing, she's dead anyway.' Spector wet his lips nervously. 'You see, Frank, this death-threat thing . . . Look, handled properly, this thing could be good for a million dollars' worth of free publicity.'

Frank Farmer moved so quickly Spector never had a chance to see it coming. The bodyguard's right hand lashed out, closed around Sy Spector's throat and slammed him up against the wall. Farmer thrust his face up close to Spector's.

'One word about this –' He spoke in a hoarse, angry whisper.

'It could clinch her nomination,' Spector managed to gasp.

'If one word about this gets into print, if there is the slightest whisper . . .' Farmer left his threat unspoken but Spector got the message loud and clear.

He nodded. 'I get it.'

Farmer relaxed his grip. 'Just remember what I said.'

Spector rubbed his bruised throat. 'Trouble with you is you don't understand the sympathy vote.'

Frank Farmer ignored him. He had already turned his attention back to the stage. There was moment of silence as the last notes of the song died away, followed by a roar and a tumultuous storm of applause. Flash-bulbs exploded like flares in the darkness and seemed to be reflected in Rachel's dazzling, bright smile. She could feel the adoration flowing out of the audience, a stimulant providing a high stronger and more exhilarating than anything a drug could provide.

Rachel fired a look at Frank, flashing him a naughty, mischievous smile. She was comfortable now, reveling in the worship of her fans.

She snatched the microphone off the stand and prowled around the stage. 'You like that? Would you like to hear another? Let me check with the boss.' She looked into the far wing. 'Billy? Okay with you?'

Billy Thomas, owner of the Mayan, nodded approval.

Rachel smiled. 'He says okay.'

The delight of the crowd was apparent, loud and throaty. The music changed to a light dance beat and the curtains behind Rachel parted, displaying a huge diamond vision screen. A video camera tracked her around the stage, throwing Rachel's image up on the screen.

'I think my feet are trying to tell me something . . . Wanna see a new video?'

The crowd erupted with joy. They were moving with her, swaying with the music.

'I want to dance!' Rachel yelled.

The video exploded on to the screen, Rachel with her dancers going through the routine Frank had seen in rehearsal the first day he had shown up at the mansion. The theater was alive, overflowing with music and motion.

Rachel skittered to the edge of the stage, close to the outstretched hands of her fans. The crowd surged forward, delirious that she was so close to them. She was baiting them, teasing them with her presence.

Two of the Mayan security guards appeared at both ends of the stage. Frank could see that they were tense, well aware that two of them were no match for an excited, frenzied crowd that was on the brink of flying out of control.

The first chink in the security armor appeared. A young man clambered over the safety barrier on to the stage. One of the security guards darted out like a ballboy at a tennis match, pushing the fan back into the jungle of outstretched hands.

But the crowd was growing bolder, pushing through the barricade, their hands almost close enough to touch their idol. Frank was frantic. It hit him hard: his task was fast becoming impossible. The killer could be anywhere in that forest of bodies, waiting until he got close enough to deliver the fatal blow. Farmer's eyes darted everywhere, squinting into the lights, looking at faces, trying to recognize the assassin. He was trying to hold him – and the entire crowd – back by sheer will power.

Rachel looked at him, sensing his frustration. His helplessness seemed to intoxicate her, egging her on, pushing her closer to danger. Boldly she strutted up to the very lip of the stage. A man jumped from the audience, scrambling up on to the stage to join her.

That was too much. Frank started foward, but Rachel waved him back. She started to dance with the man, her body swaying erotically, bumping and grinding, sinking to her knees as if adoring him. The crowd screamed, loud and shrill.

Spector slapped Farmer on the back. "Look at her! She's fucking great!' His voice was triumphant, defiant.

Frank did not think it was great. He raised his hand and spoke into the Surv-Kit. 'Henry, you there?'

'I'm on the other side of the stage. Next to Billy.'

Farmer glanced across the brightly lit space and saw his assistant. Henry waved.

Frank nodded. 'Get ready to get out. Go out and get the car ready. We've got to get her out of here.'

'Check, Frank.' Henry vanished from the wings, making for the stage door.

The dancer on stage with Rachel broke the final taboo. He reached out and grabbed her around her slim waist, spinning her gleefully. One of the beefy security guards was off and running, dashing out into the confusion to extricate her from the clutches of the fan. He slammed up against the two of them, knocking the man away, but the force of impact sent Rachel flying – out into the audience, falling into the adoring arms of a half a dozen fans.

It didn't seem possible, but the crowd became even more frenzied. Rachel out among her public! This was the kind of stunt that she was famous for in the old days, when she was just starting out, when superstardom was a vision that could only be glimpsed far off on the horizon.

There was a tight knot of delirious fans around Rachel, touching her, ripping at her clothes, passing her, hand over hand, deeper and deeper into the crowd. The tangle of people encircling Rachel seemed to boil as they strained to get a piece of her.

Fear had filled Rachel's face. She had gone over the edge – literally and figuratively – and the fear of a lone assassin had been replaced by the terror of the mob. She had lost control, overstepping the bounds of intimacy that existed between performer and audience, fracturing the always uneasy truce between idol and idolaters.

Tony led the security guards into the audience, wading into the sea of bodies, slamming people out of the way. They battered their way toward her like a team of lifeguards fighting a powerful surf.

Frank could see that mere brawn was not the way to extricate Rachel from the crowd. If the mob turned on them, it could easily overwhelm ordinary brute force. He grabbed a fire extinguisher and started toward the mêlée.

The first blast of foam bewildered the crowd. The second sent them scattering as if Frank were wielding a fire hose. Farmer dove into the space he had opened up, kicked aside a wild-eyed young man and seized Rachel. Tony saw him and started clearing a path to the main door of the auditorium, like a line backer blocking for the ball carrier. The burly bodyguard was knocking fans out of the way like ninepins – but there was a long way and a lot of people between him and the exit.

Frank knew in an instant that wasn't the way to go. 'No, Tony, no! Not here!'

But Tony saw his chance to demonstrate his superior strength, to win the day, to be the big hero. 'I'll take care of this,' he yelled, laying out a spectator with a single bruising punch to the jaw. 'Just follow me!' Then he put his head down and charged for the door like a bull.

He flailed his way through the crowd and smashed through the doors, blasting out into the crowd that was still gathered on the sidewalk. It was raining now and the cool rain seemed to have a calming effect on the throng.

Tony was exultant. He held the door open. 'Make way here!' he shouted to the milling pack of people. 'Outta the way!' A path opened to the curb – but there was no waiting limo.

Tony turned and looked back into the crowd in the theater. Not only was there no limo in front of him but Rachel and Frank were not behind him either.

He dashed out into the street, into the heavy curtain of pouring rain – just in time to see the Cadillac racing away from the Mayan, tires screeching on the wet tarmac.

'Hey!' shouted Tony. 'What the fuck? Farmer! Farmer! Come back here!'

Frank Farmer heard the bellowing bodyguard but didn't tell Henry to slow down. He looked over his shoulder at Rachel. She was huddled alone in the center of the wide back seat, tiny and doll-like. She raised her quivering hands to her face and sobbed.

Frank turned away, not wanting to stare at her. He felt uncomfortable and ill at ease. He had failed his first big test, and Rachel was now an emotional wreck.

Henry's eyes darted to the mirror and then back to the rain-slicked street.

'She's never done that before,' he said quietly.

'It's been a long night,' said Frank wearily. 'For all of us.'

Frank Farmer helped Rachel out of the car and into the house, assisting her up the stairs.

'Frank,' she whispered, 'I was so scared.'

'A good night's sleep and you'll feel better. Try not to worry about it. You're safe here.'

'Fletcher,' she said faintly. 'I have to see if he's okay.' Frank led her along the corridor at the top of the stairs and opened the door to Fletcher's room. The little boy lay in bed, sound asleep, a picture of peace. 'See? He's fine.'

Rachel looked relieved. She stole quietly into the room and kissed him gently on the forehead. Fletcher frowned in his sleep and turned over. She smiled slightly as she left the room.

'Tell me he'll always be safe,' she said.

'I give you my word.' He took her by the hand. 'C'mon. You have to get to bed.'

In her bedroom – her real one, not the showy room that Sy Spector had mocked up for the media – Frank moved quickly to check the windows. The security locks had been installed, and it was apparent that they had not been tampered with.

Rachel was standing in the middle of the bedroom, dazed and, it seemed, completely defeated by the zip on her dress. She twisted her arms behind her back and fiddled with the fastener as if it were a piece of complicated machinery entirely beyond her ken.

Farmer unclasped her dress and felt it go loose around her body, then he slipped his arm around her waist, guiding her toward the bed. She seemed very frail in his arms. Her bones felt thin and delicate, as if he could snap them with his hands. Terror and shock, the dread of death, had blown away the old, self-confident Rachel Marron and replaced her with this scared, fragile child.

Frank swept away the little dolls that were scattered on Rachel's pillows and pulled down the covers. Gently he pushed her down until she was sitting on the bed and pulled off the soiled, torn dress. She sat, docile and naked, until he guided her in between the crisp, clean sheets.

Rachel's head sank into the soft pillows and she sighed, as if she finally felt safe. Frank straightened the bedclothes and was preparing to leave her when she reached out and took his hand, grasping it the way a little girl might hold the hand of her father. Farmer stroked her hair.

'Aren't you going to ask me why I behave the way I do?' she asked in a small, tired voice.

Frank shook his head. 'I know why,' he said.

They did not speak again and he stayed with her until she fell asleep.

★

The house was silent, and Frank Farmer, still pumped up by the action of the evening and consequently unable to sleep, sat at the rough-hewn oak refectory table in the spacious kitchen. He had stripped off his jacket and tie and was slumped in the chair in his sweat-stained, dirty white shirt. He was eating a peach, carefully paring slices from the fruit with a small, sharp kitchen knife.

Frank's mind kept on slipping back to his last words to Rachel that night. Did he really know why she acted as she did? He thought so and the events of the evening seemed to confirm his theory. Or, rather, theories.

Deep down, she was a child who needed to be the center of attention; she was insecure, uncertain of her talent, and she craved the perpetual adoration of the crowd; she was a driven performer who had to dominate the stage and her whole industry; she was a courageous young woman who needed to challenge constantly – challenge herself, her fans, the people around her.

The kitchen door flew open and a gust of wet wind blew into the room. Tony stalked in. He had just made his way home from the free-for-all at the Mayan and he was boiling mad.

'You fuckin' left me there,' he growled. His big hands curled into fists.

'I had to get Rachel out of there,' said Frank, hardly looking up from his peach.

'The hell you did. If you had followed me out, we woulda been outta there.'

'It was too risky.'

'Shit on that! You just wanted the glory.'

'I don't do this for the glory,' said Frank softly.

'The hell you don't.'

Tony was in no mood for rational argument. He charged for Frank, his fists up. Farmer waited until he was almost upon him. As Tony reached for his shirt front, Frank spun out of his chair, throwing his weight against Tony's tree-trunk legs, low-bridging him, cutting his legs out from under him.

Tony fell heavily, smacking his head on the terracotta floor. Farmer was on him instantly, grabbing the chair he was sitting on. He pinned him to the floor with the legs, like a lion tamer keeping a big cat at bay.

'Tony, it's been a long night. Enough, okay?'

Tony glared up at him, but he was trapped. 'Enough,' he snarled.

'Okay.' Farmer took his weight off the chair. Tony stood up slowly, scowling.

But it seemed that he hadn't had enough. The instant he was on his feet, he threw a punch, a wide roundhouse right, his fist traveling straight at Frank's jaw.

There was a lot of power behind the punch, but the big man was slow and he was standing flat-footed, putting all his weight into the blow, trying to take Frank out in a single move. Farmer slipped under the punch, broke through Tony's guard. He waded in, landing two hard, bone-crunching jabs to the ribs. Tony tottered back and fell against the wooden kitchen cabinets that lined the walls of the room.

His back to the wall, Tony grabbed a long carving knife out of the butcher's block on the counter and held it in front of him, waving it at Frank, taunting and threatening.

Farmer sighed and shook his head. He was getting irritated now. He picked up the paring knife he had used on the peach and flipped it in his hand, catching it and holding it by the blade. Then he reached back and with a graceful, fluid motion launched the knife. The tip thudded into the cabinet less than an inch from Tony's ear.

Tony looked at the quivering blade for a moment, then lowered his own knife.

'Listen to me,' said Farmer like a firm headmaster lecturing a recalcitrant schoolboy. 'Are you paying attention?'

Tony nodded.

'Good.' Frank folded his arms. 'I'm warning you, Tony. I don't want to talk about this again.'

The cleaning crew was beginning mopping-up operations at the Mayan, a dozen men fanning out through the wrecked club with brooms and buckets. Billy Thomas was standing on the stage surveying the damage that had been done. The light was low, but the destruction was plain to see. Furniture was in splinters, the floor was littered with debris and broken glass, light fixtures had been torn from the walls.

There were still a few die-hard Rachel Marron fans hanging around, standing in little knots talking about the near-riot, exchanging stories of the rumpus, still excited by the uproar they had witnessed and had been part of. Two of the fans were still high on the experience – they had actually touched Rachel Marron.

Neither the fans nor the maintenance squad paid any attention to the lone man who was slowly walking around the auditorium, staring at the floor as if looking for something.

If challenged, he had already planned to say that he had dropped his wallet in the fracas and he was trying to find it. A perfectly plausible story . . .

But he was searching for something else and, after a while, he found it. In a little pile of torn paper and other wreckage was a scrap of material, a little rag, a bit of Rachel's dress. He knelt down next to the piece of cloth, picked it up and, furtively, held it to his nose and breathed deeply. The fabric had been held by a hundred hands and trampled under foot, but to his delight, through the dirt and the smell of sweat he could just make out the sweet odor of Rachel Marron's scent.

CHAPTER ELEVEN

Frank Farmer did not expect to see Rachel the next day – and he understood her reticence perfectly. Man-handling by hundreds of frenzied strangers would try the nerves of the calmest, most serene individuals. It must have been hell on a highly strung, emotional person like Rachel. Frank didn't imagine he would see much of her for at least a week.

He was wrong. He had checked on the early-morning guards on the gate and was walking back to the house through the quiet, dew-dampened grounds, the low morning mist swirling. A twig snapped behind him and he turned quickly.

Rachel, dressed in a soft blue running suit, came jogging along the garden path. She stopped in front of him, panting slightly. Despite the trauma of the night before, her eyes were clear and she looked relaxed and well rested. Frank could see that she was a survivor, that she could take a blow and heal quickly. He found himself admiring her.

She flashed him a knowing smile, as if she could read his thoughts. 'Hey, gotcha, didn't I?'

'Yep,' he said, smiling back.

'You're probably wondering what I'm doing?' She gestured toward her running clothes. 'You didn't know I jogged, did you?'

Frank shook his head.

'What's the matter? Afraid I'll get picked off in my snazzy running suit?'

'No,' he said slowly. 'Worse than that.'

She looked puzzled. 'Worse? What could be worse than that?'

'I'm afraid I'll have to jog with you.'

Rachel laughed. 'That's great,' she said. 'I guess that I can't do it then. I've been looking for an excuse to quit.'

'That's a relief.'

'Walk me back to the house, will you?'

'With pleasure.'

They strolled through the grounds slowly, not speaking for a while, feeling the sun strengthen to burn off the mist.

Rachel broke the silence. 'I know this is kind of late,' she said hesitantly. It appeared that she was having trouble finding the right words to say. 'I just wanted to say thank you,' she blurted out. 'I'm really glad you're here. It all makes sense now.'

'That's good.'

'I'm going to try to cooperate.'

Frank smiled. 'That's even better.'

They walked a few more yards in silence. When Rachel finally began to speak again, she sounded genuinely unsure of herself, shy and embarrassed.

'Farmer . . . I have this problem. This minor little problem.' She stammered a little, as if her own words made her nervous. Frank found this new Rachel Marron very appealing.

'What is it?'

'Well, you see, I'd like to go out for an evening. Just me and a guy . . .' She screwed her face up in a grimace, as if to excuse her embarrassing words. '. . . like a "date". But I can't go out on a date because you have to be with me every minute. I mean, what if he invited me up to his place afterward? Are you going to come too?'

'I can see the problem,' said Frank.

'Yeah, but I've thought about it and the only thing I can figure out is for *you* to take me out.'

'Me?'

'So . . . that's what I was wondering . . . you know. What do you think? But only if you want to.'

She gazed at him, her eyes full of hope. He seemed bemused by her coltish chagrin.

'Is this an order?' he asked.

'No, no, no! It's only if you want to . . . I'm really not so bad . . .'

She ran a hand through her hair and laughed nervously. 'Oh, my God, listen to me! I'm begging. This is just like being in high school again – only worse . . .' She stopped and looked at him. 'God, this is so embarrassing. Okay, this is what I'm going to do. I'm gonna run up ahead there. You decide . . .'

But before she could run away, Nicki threw open the window of the house. 'Rachel! Sandy Harris is on the phone. Says it's urgent.'

'Tell her she'll have to wait, babe,' Rachel shouted back. 'I'm getting fixed up here.'

Without a word, Nicki closed the window and vanished.

'So, Farmer, what do you say?'

'Frank.'

'Well, what do you say, *Frank*.'

'I say yes.'

The broad prow of the Cadillac limousine emerged from the car-wash tunnel like a submarine boiling up from the bottom of the sea. Soapy water sluiced off the windows and hood. A couple of car-wash workers, one black man, one white, fell on the soaked car and started working over the shiny paintwork with chamois cloths.

Henry stood idly by, bored, waiting for them to finish with the car. Frank Farmer may have promoted him to assistant bodyguard, but he was still the chauffeur and the chauffeur had to see that the cars got washed and hot waxed.

Henry hardly saw the men laboring over the car – they were just guys doing a boring, dirty job, working for minimum wage, plus tips – he didn't even notice their names embroidered on their overalls, Jamal and Dan.

But Dan, the white guy, recognized Henry. He had been at the Rachel Marron concert at the Mayan – he was the wild-eyed man whom Frank had unceremoniously kicked to one side – and he reasoned that if Henry had brought a car in, then the car must belong to the superstar herself. This interested him.

Dan tossed aside his cloth, picked up the suction hose of the industrial-strength vacuum cleaner and threw open the rear door of the limousine.

'Hey!' said Henry. 'I didn't ask for interior cleaning.'

'Relax, man,' muttered Dan, 'it's included.'

'Oh,' said Henry and thought no more about it.

Dan ran the nozzle over the thick carpeting and deep in the crevices in the crushed velour upholstery. Under one of the seats the tube sucked up a crumpled ball of paper, too big, too thick to fit down the pipe. Dan smoothed it out on the soft rear seat and saw that it was a signed publicity picture of Rachel Marron, the kind of thing stars gave out by the handful.

Impassively, Dan folded the picture and slid it into his overall pocket. He backed out of the passenger compartment and turned off the vacuum cleaner.

'All done,' he said.

'Great,' said Henry. He slapped a ten-dollar bill in

the hand of both cleaners, got behind the wheel and drove off.

'Good tip,' said Jamal.

'Yeah,' said Dan. He walked away from the wash bay and went directly to his locker in the employees' changing room. He spun through the numbers on the combination lock and pulled open the door of the battered metal box.

Pasted over every inch of the interior of the locker were pictures of Rachel Marron. There were publicity stills and pictures clipped from magazines and newspapers, album covers and smaller versions snipped from CD boxes. In the center of the collection, displayed like a holy relic, was the scrap of cloth retrieved the night before from the debris-strewn floor of the Mayan. The whole compartment looked like a shrine to Rachel Marron – except for one small detail. Scrawled across one of the larger photographs of a smiling Rachel Marron was a single, angry word: *Whore.*

Of the hundred or so devotees of Japanese cinema who assembled in the Kokusai Theater that night, approximately ninety-eight of them were unaware that Rachel Marron was in the audience among them. It was a secret shared by Frank and Rachel alone.

Her disguise had not been all that elaborate – a hat and a silk scarf wound high around her neck – and a pair of sun glasses that she took off only when the movie was about to begin.

Frank Farmer may not have known much about popular culture, but he knew a good movie when he saw one – and Akiro Kurosawa's *Yojimbo* was one of the best.

The great Japanese actor Toshiro Mifune, who

played the part of a cynical samurai for hire who engineers the bloody destruction of an entire town, was riveting. Rachel, who had never seen a Japanese movie before, sat in the dark transfixed by the story, hardly moving from the opening shot of Mifune, photographed from behind against a backdrop of high snow-capped mountains, to the last ironic line: 'Now we'll have quiet in this town.'

Rachel was thoughtful as they walked out of the theater. 'Well,' she said pensively, 'he didn't look like he wanted to die to me.'

'Well, he didn't die, did he? There's a big difference between wanting to die and having no fear of death.'

They were walking on the sidewalk now, heading for Frank Farmer's unostentatious Chevrolet. They could have been any couple out on a date.

'And because he had no fear of death,' she said, 'that made him invincible?'

'What do you think?'

Rachel smiled. 'Well, one thing's for sure – he creamed them all in the end.'

Frank nodded. 'Yeah, it was a good movie.'

'How many times have you seen it?'

'Sixty-two,' he said without missing a beat.

Rachel chuckled. 'You have any idea what *Yojimbo* means?'

Frank hesitated a moment. 'Yeah . . .'

'What? Tell me?'

'It means "the bodyguard".'

Rachel let loose a peal of delighted laughter. 'Well, now I understand. That explains everything!'

Da Umberto's restaurant, in the anonymous, seedy suburb of Echo Park, was nothing like Morton's – it was almost, but not quite, a dive. No famous faces here. But the food was authentically Tuscan, and soft music oozed from the speaker of an old beat-up juke box in the corner. Umberto's was almost empty and there was no one out on the tiny dance floor.

Rachel was enchanted, happier than she had been in a long time. She had almost forgotten what it was like to go out just for the pleasure of it instead of for show. She was relaxed, at ease and finding herself becoming fascinated with her dinner companion.

'Your kind of place, huh?'

Frank nodded. He toyed with his *pappardelle al cervo*, moving the strands of wide pasta around on his plate.

She cocked an ear toward a speaker. 'And your kind of music?'

'Absolutely,' he said emphatically.

'Do you feel safe here? You figure no one could get by you in a place like this?' She took a bite of her own pasta.

Frank Farmer shrugged. 'If someone is willing to swap his life for a kill, nothing can stop him.'

Rachel smiled ruefully. 'Great. What do I need you for?'

'He might get me instead.' It wasn't a boast, a macho man thumping his chest. It was a simple statement of fact.

Her eyes widened. 'And you're ready to die for me?'

'That's my job,' he said.

Rachel stared hard at him, as if answers could be read in his calm face. 'And you'd do it? Why?'

Frank smiled slightly. 'Because I can't sing.'

'*Yo*-jimbo,' said Rachel and laughed.

'No, he was better than I am.'

She waved off his modesty. 'That's just the magic of the movies, Farmer. You – you're the real thing.'

Frank shrugged and poured them both a little more wine.

'Something I don't understand . . .'

'What's that?'

'Well, maybe there's some glory in saving a president or something, but just anyone . . .'

'You mean like you? It's a matter of conditioning and discipline.'

Rachel frowned and shook her head. 'I don't trust discipline – not mine, anyway. At the crucial moment I know I'd cop out.'

'That happens.'

'But not with you, Fierce Frank.' Rachel laughed softly. 'Your discipline is always working for you, right?'

'No one can ever predict what would happen in a life-or-death situation. Let's just say it happens and leave it at that.'

They were quiet while the waiter cleared their plates, as if they didn't want a stranger eavesdropping on their secret, intimate conversation.

'Tell me . . . have you ever liked anybody?'

'What do you mean?' He knew exactly what she meant but he was far from happy at having to relinquish information so personal. It was second nature to Frank Farmer to play his cards close to his chest. To keep his personal life personal.

'Like me . . .'

Frank laughed out loud, an unusual reaction for a man like him. 'I've never known anyone like you.'

'You know what I mean. Like me – a girl.'

He shifted uncomfortably, considering the question. She was being completely open with him – it would be good strategy, not to mention courteous, for him to return the favor. It would establish a trust between them that would allow him to protect her that much better. There was a red line, though, that he knew he couldn't cross.

'There was a girl,' he said looking beyond her. 'A long time ago.'

'There was? What happened? You don't mind if I ask, do you?'

'You don't mind if I don't answer, do you?' he shot back with a smile.

'I . . . I don't want to pry . . .'

Frank Farmer's smile widened. Rachel was one of the nosiest people he had ever met in his life.

Rachel started to laugh, unable to help herself. 'She didn't die, did she?' she asked giddily. 'I mean, you weren't, like . . . protecting her and she got killed?'

Frank's smile vanished. His face closed, grim and somber. His silence spoke volumes.

Rachel stopped laughing in mid-chuckle. She immediately looked stricken and she paled slightly. 'Oh, my God! That's it, isn't it?'

Frank's voice was bleak, the look on his face serious and solemn. 'Well, nobody's perfect,' he said.

Rachel was taken aback, shocked and mortified by her own insensitivity. She had abruptly changed the mood, casting a cold, dark shadow over the evening. 'Oh, Frank, I'm so sorry,' she gasped.

Then it was as if someone had switched on a bright light. The solemnity in his face disappeared and he laughed easily. 'No, she didn't get killed . . .' He paused a moment, as if not sure how to go on. 'It was less dramatic than that,' he said finally. 'She just didn't love me anymore. Can you imagine a thing like that?'

Rachel looked him square in the eye. 'No,' she said evenly, 'not really.'

The song on the juke box ended and there was a moment of silence. Then another record dropped on to the turntable. Then came the opening strains of 'What Becomes of the Broken-hearted'. It was one of Rachel Marron's earliest hits, the song that propelled her into the spotlight once and for all. Frank smiled when he heard her voice. He raised his wine glass, toasting her and her breakthrough song.

'So,' she said a little smile playing on her lips, 'is this a full service date, Frank?'

Frank looked warily at her, gazing over the top of his glass.

'I'm just asking you to dance.'

'My pleasure,' he said.

Frank never failed to astonish her. For such a seemingly buttoned-up personality, he was a smooth, graceful dancer and he seemed perfectly at ease holding her, being close. It was not something she would have imagined he would be comfortable with. She rested her head on his shoulder and hummed along with her own voice.

Frank could smell the perfume in her hair and felt her moving supple and sensual in his strong arms. They were both listening to the lyrics of the sad song, Rachel's silky smooth phrasing bringing real sorrow to the melancholy words She raised her head from his shoulder and looked at him. 'You like this? The song, I mean.'

Frank nodded. 'Yeah.'

Rachel burst out laughing and Frank colored slightly, embarrassed, afraid that he had said something humiliating.

'What? What are you laughing at?'

Rachel tried to compose herself. 'I'm sorry.' She giggled. 'It's just that this song . . . It's so depressing.'

Frank grinned. 'It is, isn't it?'

From the kitchen of the restaurant came an intrusive noise, the loud crash of a load of crockery hitting the floor and shattering. Without even thinking about it, Frank made a smooth, quick turn, putting his body between Rachel and the noise. He looked over his shoulder, seeking out the source of the sound, just to make sure there was no danger.

Rachel laid her head on his shoulder again. 'Don't worry,' she whispered in his ear. 'I'll protect you.'

They drifted back into the music, Rachel singing to herself, lost in thought, lost in his arms. Frank's eyes were open and alert, ever vigilant.

CHAPTER TWELVE

Just as there was a private place in Frank Farmer's heart, so there was a place in his modest home that was usually off-limits to outsiders. He had fitted out the basement of his house as a gym and workshop, doing all the remodeling himself, paneling the bare block walls and laying down a smooth tile floor on the cold cement.

In one corner there was a collection of gleaming, chrome-plated exercise equipment, a stack of weights and boxing gear, a speed bag and a heavy bag. In another part of the large room was a workbench with dozens of tools, each meticulously labeled and stored, along with some heavier machinery – a lathe and a drill press – where he did metal work, modifying the weapons that were the tools of his trade.

The most unusual part of the cellar was partitioned off from the rest of the room, a narrow, sound-proofed corridor running the length of the wall. It was a private shooting range with a target tacked to a stack of sandbags at the far end.

The whole room had an unfussy order about it, a placid, simple plainness coupled with an air of unerring yet unobtrusive efficiency – not unlike Farmer himself.

He sat on the couch, sipping a drink, watching her. Rachel prowled the room, touching the tools on the bench and peering down the long shooting gallery.

'It's very quiet here,' she said, almost to herself. She walked to the wall of books and trophies that covered one side of the room. The books were an odd collection of volumes – novels stood next to technical manuals, thick biographies and histories leaned against large picture books, lavish volumes on wild flowers, weapons, Japanese cinema and primitive art.

The books told Rachel that Farmer had a lively intellect and a curiosity about a wide range of different subjects, but she knew that already. More interesting were the few personal mementoes dotted about, here and there, on the shelves. There were dusty trophies, framed citations, photographs: Frank being presented with his black belt, a very young Frank in a baseball batting cage, his bat cocked in a mean stance. There were pictures of him with three presidents.

Rachel picked up one of the pictures and angled it toward the light. It was a group photo of a football squad, the teammates staring into the lens of the camera with the profound seriousness of the very young. She read off the printed inscription that ran along the bottom of the picture.

'West Virginia University Football.' Rachel scanned the ranks of stern faces until she found him. She looked up and smiled. 'God, look at you.'

'It was a long time ago.'

'I didn't know you played football.'

'I don't – not anymore.'

'What did you play? What position?'

'End,' he said.

'Were you tough?' she asked with a smile.

'No. Fast.'

Surmounting the mementoes, hanging on the wall, was the long, slim black-lacquer scabbard of a Japanese sword. Rachel peered at it closely, touching the buttery smooth finish lightly.

'You some kind of samurai too?'

Frank smiled. 'That requires real discipline.'

'They said you were in the Secret Service. What made you get out?'

'Money.'

Rachel looked around the austere, sparsely furnished room and smiled. 'I can see that your tastes are extravagant.'

She turned back to the sword. 'May I?'

Frank nodded and she took the scabbard off its mount and began to slide the sword out of the case.

'Watch yourself,' he cautioned.

The naked blade was breathtakingly beautiful, the steel buffed to a flawless shine. The gentle curve of the shaft was perfectly balanced, as graceful as a ray of light. She held the sword out in front of her and walked to where he sat.

'You're a hard one to figure, Frank Farmer.' She stepped closer to him, the point of the blade level with his eyes, only a foot from his face. 'It seems to me,' she said, 'a bodyguard must know a little peace.'

Frank stood, the point of the blade now only an inch from his chest. He reached across the sword to Rachel's neck and untied the silk scarf she was wearing. With one hand he gently pulled off the scarf, the other hand lingering on the arch of her neck for a moment.

'Watch this,' he murmured.

He raised the scarf over his head. With both hands he spread out the filmy material and then let it fall. Slowly, billowing, the diaphanous silk floated down to the blade. As it touched it, the razor-sharp edge of the shaft bit into the delicate cloth, cutting the scarf in two pieces.

Frank reached for Rachel, pushing aside the sword. As they sank slowly to the floor, her body melted into his and they kissed.

Their lovemaking was fevered at first, as ardent as if after weeks of denial they were finally giving in, slaking desire that had built up like steam. It had been too long for both of them, and neither was prepared for the initial intensity of the experience. Then, as the night progressed, the pace of their passion slowed slightly and their lovemaking took on a more languorous, lazier rhythm, a more leisurely pace.

Deep in the night, lying naked under the sheets on Frank's bed, Rachel snuggled into his arms, her hands on his chest. 'I've never felt this safe before,' she whispered.

Frank did not answer. He merely smiled and stroked her disheveled hair.

'No one could get by you.'

'Right now it might not be so hard.'

Rachel laughed and kissed him, then buried her head in his shoulder. 'I'm not worried,' she said.

He listened to the measure of her breathing slow as she fell asleep. He remained awake for a little while longer, staring in the dark.

She wakened to the sharp rasp of the blinds being raised. The stark bedroom was flooded with light. She sat up and blinked.

'What? What is it? What are you doing?'

Frank was dressed in suit trousers and a white shirt. He was knotting a tie at his throat. His chest was girded with the leather straps of a shoulder holster, the pocket empty. One look at his face and she knew there was something terribly wrong. He appeared angry, enraged. He didn't answer her.

'Frank?'

Farmer wouldn't look at her. 'Rachel, I don't want to get confused about what I'm doing here.' The moment he had opened his eyes that morning the enormity of what he had done struck him like a heavy weight. He had been weak, and his weakness had endangered them both. His anger was intense, but it was directed inward, at his own foolishness, not at Rachel.

'Confused?' she said. She sounded bewildered by his harsh words. 'I'm not confused.'

'You pay me to protect you. That's what I do.'

'So? Have I done something wrong? What did I do?'

'Nothing. It's not you.'

'Then what is it?' She lifted the sheet seductively and looked at him, a small, mischievous smile on her lips. He looked away.

'Do you want me to beg?' she demanded.

'No,' he said curtly. 'I want you to do without.'

She shook her head and her brow furrowed. 'What's going on, Frank?'

'I want to keep it straight in my head what job I'm doing.' He stared fixedly at the floor as he spoke, as if concentrating on the words, memorizing them.

'And what is that exactly? Making me feel like shit?'

He passed a hand across his forehead. He hadn't intended his words to sound so blunt. Hurting her was the last thing he wanted to do, particularly after last night. 'You didn't do anything. It was me. I involved myself with a client.'

'A "client"?' The impersonal word stung her. 'That's all I am to you, your *client*?'

'I made a mistake.' Frank spoke in a low monotone. Inside, he cursed himself for his rashness. A bodyguard in love with the woman he was supposed to protect was almost as dangerous as the assassin himself.

'What mistake? You don't find me attractive anymore. Is that it?'

Frank's anger caught fire. 'Christ! I've told you why. I can't protect you like this. I'm no good to you.'

'And so what does that mean?' she fired back. 'That's it for me? One night and it's over?'

Frank nodded. 'That's right.'

Rachel rolled her eyes, as if asking heaven to explain this weird turn of events. 'I don't believe it.'

He opened the drawer of the night table on his side of the bed and took out his gun, automatically checking it before sliding it into his shoulder holster. 'You can live with that or you can fire me.'

'But I can't fuck you,' she snapped.

Frank turned and looked at her, pain in his eyes. Couldn't she see that this was hard for him too? 'I'm sorry,' he said softly.

'I don't believe this.' She was silent a moment, thinking about what was happening to her. A few hours earlier she thought she had found security and happiness. Now he was taking it all away, as quickly and as casually as it had been offered. 'I'm asking you . . . Let me tell you . . .'

Suddenly, self-pity was replaced with a hot flash of anger. *He* was rejecting *her*. That was not the kind of treatment Rachel Marron was used to.

'Just what the hell do you think you're doing?'

'I'm doing what's right. I'm doing what's right for both of us.'

Rachel stared at him for moment, as if she didn't understand the meaning of the words he had spoken. Then, abruptly, with a roar of frustration, humiliation and rage, she lurched from the bed, diving for her clothes. Frank shut his eyes tight, trying to fight off the waves of mortification and pain that broke over him.

CHAPTER THIRTEEN

An early-morning mist rose off the swimming pool at Rachel Marron's estate. Frank knelt at the water's edge, Fletcher next to him, the little boy watching as Frank loaded fresh batteries into the radio-remote-controlled speedboat. Farmer was preoccupied with the events of the night before and that morning, and Fletcher could see the worry clear as day.

'She's real mad at you, isn't she?'

Frank stopped and stared blankly at the batteries in his hand, as if, for a moment, he didn't know what they were. His silence spoke volumes.

'She told me that she doesn't understand why you're so shitty to her. You're supposed to be our friend.'

Farmer's shoulders drooped and he breathed out an almost imperceptible sigh. 'I *am* your friend,' he said, without looking up. He resumed his task, sliding the batteries into place.

'Then what's going on?'

'I've spent a lot of time learning not to react to things other people do,' he explained, hoping that his words would get through to the child, that they would make sense. 'It's my job. I have to be disciplined.' He sighed again. 'But it doesn't always work, Fletcher. It doesn't always work.'

Fletcher shook his head. 'I don't get it. I don't think I understand, Frank.'

Frank smiled and shrugged. 'I'm an old man compared to you, pal, and I don't understand either. And I'm starting to get the feeling I never will.'

There was a crunch of footsteps on the gravel path that led down to the pool. Nicki was carrying an armful of magazines and newspapers and bundles of that morning's mail.

'Ta-daaa!' She let a copy of *Daily Variety*, the show-business industry newspaper, fall to the ground. 'Take a look,' she said. 'The votes are in.'

The thick black headline read: 'AND THE NOMINEES ARE . . .' Rachel's name was prominent among them.

'Mom made it!' said Fletcher happily.

Nicki gazed at Frank curiously, taunting him with her eyes. She was the first to realize that morning that Rachel's bed had not been slept in.

'I thought you'd like to know about the nomination. Everyone said she was a sure thing. Of course, you know all about that,' she said, her voice heavy with irony.

If she had expected him to be embarrassed, she was mistaken.

'What's that supposed to mean?' He looked back at her, his gaze steady.

She looked away. 'I'm sorry. That was out of line. It's none of my business.' She held out the mail. 'Here are today's question marks for you.'

Without a word he took the mail, and she turned and walked briskly back to the house, as if anxious to get away.

'You seem to be upsetting everybody today, Frank,' Fletcher observed.

'It's a gift.'

Fletcher laughed and launched his boat on the deep blue water.

One of the first orders Frank had given was that no

parcels were to be opened until he had had a chance to examine them. He had taken over a utility room off the garage where the cleaning staff stored their equipment, outfitting it as a small lab where he could examine suspicious packages without endangering the people in the house. Among the mail Nicki had given him that morning was a small box, a container not much bigger than a pack of cigarettes.

Frank held the package over the deep concrete sink, a solid basin he had filled with loose sand and had further fortified, stacking heavy sandbags up above the edge of the tub. He investigated the carton with the care of a surgeon, listening to it with a stethoscope and running it through a metal detector. It had been addressed in the normal way, except that Rachel's name had been cut out of a magazine and pasted above the scrawled address, possibly a clue that their man had gotten in touch once again.

The metal detector registered nothing and the stethoscope picked up no tell-tale ticking. But that told him nothing; any bomb maker worth his salt these days used silent, solid-state quartz timers.

Very carefully he sliced the covering brown paper with a straight razor and stripped off the outer wrap. He took a deep breath and opened the box. Inside was a tight wad of newspaper protecting an item within. Using a pair of tweezers, he started unraveling the packing cautiously, aware that the merest careless move might detonate a bomb.

There was a loud metallic click, then a loud buzzing, and the paper moved slightly. Instantaneously Frank dropped the package into the sink and hit the floor, covering his head with his hands, waiting for the explosion.

He lay stretched on the concrete for a few seconds –

it felt like an eternity – listening to the hum as it slowly wound down.

Silence.

Guardedly Frank got to his feet and peered into the sink. The package was still. He sniffed the air, no smoke from a misfired detonator. Holding his breath, he extracted the wad of paper and unwrapped it quickly. Inside the box was a mechanical toy, a wind-up beaver with a gaily colored hand-painted sign around its neck: 'WE LOVE YOU, RACHEL! FROM YOUR DEVOTED FANS IN BEAVER PENNSYLVANIA – SALLY AND KATE.'

Frank put the toy down on the table and the beaver's plastic teeth chattered mockingly. Frank exhaled mightily and tried to relax. A nerve-racking little incident like that probably shortened his life by ten years. He held his right arm straight out, palm downwards, and looked at it. No tremor.

Henry appeared in the doorway of the room. 'What the hell are you doing, Frank?'

'Just checking.'

'Oh. Sy Spector wants to see you in the office.'

Frank Farmer's shoulders sagged. 'Great. That's all I need.'

Spector may have asked to see him, but he didn't seem happy as Frank walked in. He sat behind a desk in the production office that Rachel maintained in the house, his scowling face in marked contrast to the huge arrangements of flowers and bunches of floating helium balloons that seemed to fill the office. These were gifts from the rest of Hollywood, a traditional way of congratulating an Oscar nominee. In the small room beyond the office two secretaries were busy answering the constantly ringing phone as industry people, friends and enemies alike, called in their best wishes for Rachel. It was protocol, a strict show-business convention.

Spector was in no mood for argument. 'Put together a list of your expenses. Your total billings. Let me have it in one hour and I'll see that a check is cut.' That was it. He went back to the paperwork on his desk.

Frank raised an eyebrow. 'Don't you ever just say what's on your mind, Spector?'

Spector exploded. He stood up, his face red, the veins in his neck standing out, as if straining to break through the taut skin. 'What's on my mind is that you're fired, Frank. She missed all her interviews yesterday because of your little date. Do you realize she stood up Barbara Walters?'

Not showing up for an interview with the ABC newswoman was a gaffe, but it wasn't something that couldn't be repaired. Spector had shmoozed Walters and her producer into rescheduling, and everybody was happy again. More important, though, was the nomination: Sy Spector felt he deserved the lion's share of the credit for having engineered it, and that meant he was at the peak of his power in the Rachel Marron organization. He firmly believed in the old maxim about power: use it or lose it. And he was using it to get rid of a rival.

Frank found himself wondering if Henry had checked the flowers for explosives.

'First,' Spector continued, 'you fuck up her career. And now you're fucking up her head!'

'That's between us,' said Frank tersely.

'Oh, you think so? You forget who signs your check. You don't understand the role I play around here.'

'No, I understand. It's you who haven't figured things out, Spector.'

'Just what the hell is that supposed to mean?'

'You watch the bottom line, right? Make sure you get your cut of Rachel Marron?'

'Damn right I do. That's the way things work.'

'Then tell me how much money you stand to make when you're getting ten per cent of a corpse?'

'You are sick, Frank. Really sick. I feel sorry for you. Get your shit together and be out of here by noon.'

'Frank stays.'

Farmer and Spector turned to see Bill Devaney and Rachel standing in the doorway.

'I say he goes,' insisted Spector.

'Be reasonable, Sy. With this high a profile, with the nomination and the Oscars coming up, Rachel needs protection now more than ever. If Frank goes, you can forget Miami.'

Spector's anger clicked up a notch. 'Forget Miami? She's signed the fucking contract, Bill. You want me to read the goddamn thing to you?'

Rachel was watching both angry men, turning from one to another as each spoke like a spectator at a tennis match.

'Fuck the contract,' asserted Devaney. 'If he goes, she's not singing a note. It's too dangerous.'

'Oh. "Fuck the contract." Great. Why don't you let Rachel speak for herself? I think she has some say in this. Rachel, what do you say?'

Rachel looked from Spector to Devaney to Frank. 'He stays,' she said. There was no doubt in her voice.

'Mr Spector!' called one of the secretaries. 'Mr Schiller is calling. Line one.'

Spector ignored her, still looking at Devaney, Rachel and Frank. He had overplayed his hand, committing one of the worst mistakes imaginable, breaking the first command of show business: thou shalt not contradict the star.

'Well,' he said, trying to make light of his strategic miscalculation. 'I guess this is democracy in action.'

Rachel nodded. 'That's right.'

He shrugged and looked contrite, trying to worm his way back into Rachel's good graces. 'I gave in, right? That's not easy for me.' He held his arms out, open wide. 'Don't I get a hug?'

'No,' said Rachel. 'You don't.'

Spector shook his head. 'Guess I'll stay in the dog house a little longer . . .' To cover his embarrassment he turned to take the call, picking up the phone. 'Hey, Ben, how are ya? Uh-huh . . .'

'Ben Schiller is the manager at the Fontainebleau Hotel in Miami Beach,' explained Devaney.

Spector was silent a moment. 'The Ambassador? What the hell are you trying to pull, Ben? Rachel always gets the Presidential suite . . .' They could just hear Schiller's voice frantically trying to explain away the mistake. 'I don't care what you thought,' growled Spector. Here was a chance to win Rachel back, playing hard ball on her behalf, even over something as trivial as a hotel reservation.

'You know the hotel?' Devaney asked Frank.

The bodyguard nodded.

'How does the Ambassador Suite compare to the Presidential for us?'

Frank thought for a moment. 'Presidential is better. It's more isolated. Twentieth-floor penthouse, south wing. There's a service elevator right there that we could quarantine. Mainly ocean windows. Should be no problem there.'

Spector was still dealing with the manager. 'I am

aware that you have a problem, Ben. But let me remind you that you people invited us.'

'Let me,' said Rachel. 'Stick around, Farmer, we may need your vaunted expertise.' She pressed a button on the phone and the speaker came on. 'Hello, Ben, honey,' she said sweetly.

'Rachel!' Ben Schiller's voice filled the room. 'Congratulations on the nomination! You must be thrilled that your –'

Rachel cut him off. 'Ben, I hear you've got me in the annexe next to the kitchen . . .'

That night John Tesh, co-anchor of the powerful show-business TV show *Entertainment Tonight*, led with the story.

'It's off to Sun City for Best Actress nominee Rachel Marron. Rachel's giving two AIDS charity concerts this week at Miami's Fontainebleau Hotel. A thousand dollars a plate for those lucky enough to get an invite.

'And rumor has it that the lovely lady has unseated the Governor of Florida himself. Seems that there was a showdown about who would get to lounge in that big Fontainebleau penthouse. A protocol nightmare for the luxurious Miami Beach institution. Guess who won? Well, when it comes to show business or politics, who would *you* vote for? No contest, right?

'Sleep tight in the Presidential Suite, Rachel. Who says a nomination isn't as good as winning?'

CHAPTER FOURTEEN

Frank Farmer flew into Miami Beach a little ahead of Rachel and her staff because he wanted to inspect every inch of the Presidential Suite at the Fontainebleau before he would allow her to take up residence. The examination took six hours, and he was shadowed from room to room by Al Thuringer, the jowly, middle-aged head of security for the hotel.

The penthouse was made up of eight luxurious, sun-washed rooms with impressive views of the beach and the light-green ocean. As befitted a hotel apartment that cost four thousand dollars a day, the suite was appropriately sumptuous, decorated with valuable antique furniture and discreetly hidden electronic gadgets. Works of art swung away to reveal large television screens; bookshelves opened up to an array of stereo, video and laser disc systems.

A bar in a corner of the giant living room was stocked with every conceivable beverage, non-alcoholic and more potent. Frank spent an hour meticulously inspecting the cap of each and every bottle to make sure that it had not been opened.

He examined every piece of furniture and opened every drawer, sealing each of them with a piece of security tape. Dade County police brought in dogs trained to sniff for explosives and they wandered from room to room but found nothing.

It was on the balcony that Frank found the only feature that he judged to be possibly lethal. The strut supporting the railing had broken, and the cement anchoring it was dry and crumbling. Frank put his weight on it and it swayed precariously. The whole barrier was dangerously unstable, an accident waiting to happen.

'Hey, Thuringer.'

'What is it?'

Farmer put his hands on the railing and rattled the metalwork.

'Goddamn,' said the security chief in alarm. 'How the hell did that happen? I'll get someone on it right away.' He made a note on a piece of paper attached to a clipboard.

Frank nodded. 'Let's check the rest of the building. Downstairs.'

'Got ya,' said Thuringer.

They stepped into the corridor outside the front door of the suite. There were two people in the hallway, hotel employees steam-cleaning the wall-to-wall carpet. Frank looked at them suspiciously.

'It's okay,' Thuringer assured him. 'They've been checked out. They're clean.'

A small boy and his nanny emerged from the elevator. The boy was wearing a bathing suit and carried a wet towel

'Hi!' said the boy.

'Hi, Mark,' replied Thuringer. 'Been swimming?'

'Body surfing. It was great!' He ran down the hall toward the door of the only other suite on the floor.

Frank looked at the security chief quizzically. 'Who the hell are they?'

'The Katzes of St Louis,' whispered Thuringer. 'Very prominent family in the Midwest. Real estate. Oil. They come every year. An elderly couple and three grandchildren. A nurse and a maid.'

'You told me this floor would be clear.'

'C'mon, Farmer, relax. These people have more money than God. They're not going to cause any trouble.'

'I hope not.'

'They have the room at the far end of the wing. Every other room on this floor has been kept vacant. And, as you asked, we did the same with the rooms in the floor below.'

'Good.'

'Now where?'

'I want to see the theater and the kitchen downstairs.'

Thuringer held the elevator door open. 'After you.'

Few places are busier than the kitchen of a large hotel. It was mid afternoon. The luncheon rush was over, but dozens of employees were already preparing for dinner, still hours away. At the food-prep stations sous-chefs and their assistants chopped and diced vegetables. Sauciers were already sweating over hot stoves, and in the middle of it all, like a general commanding an army in the field, stood the chef, directing his troops. The din of clattering pots and pans was neverending and appliances, blenders and food processors wailed.

Frank looked at all the employees and shook his head. How could he make such a heavily populated area secure? Thuringer seemed to read his thoughts.

'We did background checks on everyone, Frank,' he shouted in Farmer's ear. 'Nothing to worry about. These people just want to keep their jobs. No one here is gonna bother your client. But just to be on the safe side, we issued special ID cards to the kitchen staff. They have to show them to a guard to get in the back door. That way no one could get in unauthorized.'

Frank appreciated the security chief's extra precaution, but he knew that there was some enlightened self-interest at work here. The hotel stood to make more money if it became known as a place that Rachel Marron favored. The flip side of the coin was that they stood to lose a lot if she happened to be murdered on the premises.

'What about explosives? You could hide a ton of plastic explosives in here.'

'Jeez, you really are jumpy.' Thuringer laughed. 'We'll get the Dade County boys back in here with the dogs. They'll do sweeps before every show. How's that?'

'That's about all we can do.'

'It won't happen, Frank. Don't worry about it.'

'Let's check the auditorium.'

In contrast to the kitchen, the auditorium was a vast, silent room. The only noise was the sound of a piano being tuned.

Frank strode out of the wings with Thuringer and they stood center-stage, looking out into the empty hall. The seats had been removed. Later the hotel staff would put up tables for the fat cats who had paid a thousand dollars for dinner and a concert, but right then the vastness of the room and the nakedness of the spot on stage where Rachel would stand bothered him. It was bare, exposed and defenseless.

He shook his head and smiled at Thuringer. 'What a silly job this is,' he said.

Rachel Marron and her hangers-on arrived in Miami Beach that afternoon to find that Sy Spector already had the publicity machine in high gear. To get some coverage on the local evening news programs, Rachel's publicist had a camera crew standing by which 'just happened' to catch the star when she decided to take a leisurely stroll around the Fontainebleau pool.

Rachel stood in the lower lobby of the hotel, just inside the glass doors that led out to the pool area, waiting for the camera crew to get in position. Frank, Sy Spector and Ben Schiller, manager of the hotel, stood with her. The bright floodlights clocked on.

'Okay,' shouted the producer of the spot. 'We're rolling, Rachel.'

Spector eased her toward the doors. 'Okay, Rachel. Let's go. It's showtime!'

Frank looked out at the sea of people clustered around the swimming pool. 'Is this really necessary?' he asked uneasily.

'Yes,' said Spector curtly. 'It is.'

'Quit bitching, Farmer,' snapped Rachel. 'This is the part you *do* get paid for.' With that, she swept through the sliding glass doors, the camera crew and her people scurrying along behind her.

The area around the pool was crowded with hundreds of guests basking in the sun, lazing on chaises-longues. It seemed to Frank Farmer that they had stepped into an ocean of sun-baked bodies stretching away toward the beach. Waiters in short white jackets darted from person to person, taking drinks orders, then hurrying to the bar to fill them.

Near the pool itself stood a tall lifeguard's chair, rising from the acre of sunburnt flesh like a skyscraper. A tanned, muscular young man lolled in the seat, idly watching the tourists in the pool. From his vantage point, he was the first to see the camera crew and the commotion. Suddenly, he sat bolt upright, craning his neck for a better view.

Frank shot a sidelong glance at Rachel, studying her face and wondering at the amazing and abrupt change that had come over her. The sunbathers around the pool had ceased to be mere tourists soaking up the tropical sun and had become an audience, a group of people that Rachel had to win over. She had to make them love her. Adrenalin pulsed through her body.

Quickly Rachel fell into an act, walking briskly among the half naked people, pretending to be shocked at the shameless display of skin. Just as shamelessly, though, she played for the camera, giving the crew what they wanted.

She came to a halt in front of a dark-haired teenage girl who was sprawled in the sun wearing a bikini that would have fitted neatly in the palm of her hand.

'Oh, my God,' gasped Rachel in mock shock. 'Look what you're wearing.' She pointed to a fat, middle-aged man a few spaces away. 'Mister, you'd better hide your eyes.'

The teenager sat up, shading her eyes against the sun and the camera lights. 'Rachel Marron!' she said, not quite able to believe her eyes.

'That's right, honey.'

'Can I have your autograph?'

'Well, sure, if you can find a piece of paper in that bathing suit of yours – which I doubt.'

'Wait! Wait!' The girl dug in the beach bag next to her seat, searching for pen and paper.

'I couldn't wear that suit . . . Honey, you're naked!' The girl laughed nervously and pressed a piece of paper into Rachel's hand.

'My name is Tracy.'

Rachel signed. 'Tracy, does your mother know you're wearing that itty-bitty thing? I guess if I had a body like that . . .' She signed the piece of paper and moved on.

There were murmurs of recognition among the

crowd now, and people in the immediate area were thrusting out their hands, as if Rachel was a politician out on the campaign trail, pressing the flesh.

'I'm a big fan.'

'That's good, honey.'

'I loved *Queen of the Night*.'

'I saw it eight times.'

'You're gonna win, Rachel.'

'Well,' she said with a laugh, 'I *sure* hope so.'

The crowd around her was getting bigger. Frank could feel the sticky warmth generated by the super-heated flesh, and his hands were slick with sun-tan oil as he warded people off, keeping a little breathing space between Rachel and the sweaty public.

To get a better view, some people stood on their chaises. Others scrambled for pens and paper. The crowd grew, and there came the sound of shattering glass as drinks trays were tipped over; furniture collapsed with a crash; flower tubs and shrubbery were trampled. On the edge of the mob there was pushing and shoving as people strained to catch a glimpse of her.

Frank managed to clear a path as far as the lifeguard station. Rachel eyed the bronzed young man appreciatively.

'You look like a man of good taste to me. You come to my party tonight . . .' She turned to Ben Schiller. 'Ben, you make sure that this boy gets into my party.'

'Anything you say, Rachel.'

She glanced past the portly hotel manager and looked at Frank, making sure he got the point: she was Rachel Marron and she could do anything she pleased – and the hell with security.

Spector leaned forward and whispered in her ear. 'Great, babe. The media got what they needed. Let's get back inside.'

'Okay.' But she lingered a moment, drinking in the whistles and the applause and the chant of 'Rachel! Rachel!' that had started on the edge of the crowd.

Frank was sweating in his suit. Things were careening out of control. A child of six or seven caught in the mob was crying loudly, frightened by the mess of legs and Bermuda shorts. Some of the older tourists looked weak and unhappy. Farmer took Rachel firmly by the arm and started propelling her back toward the lobby.

At the glass doors, she turned and flashed another sunny smile. 'Thank you all, thank you. Come tonight and hear me sing and give to the charity until it hurts.'

Frank pushed her through the open door, into the cool, air-conditioned atmosphere of the lobby, and slid the door shut. Hands and faces pressed flat against the glass and someone tried to slide the door open, an ardent fan who wanted to pursue Rachel inside. Frank locked the door, then hurried along behind Rachel and Spector.

Her public face had vanished. She slipped on a pair of sunglasses and scowled at her publicist. 'I'm beginning to wonder about your judgement, Sy. Why do I have to keep paying my dues if I've already arrived?'

Spector knew her better than she thought. He spoke very quickly. 'Kick me, beat me, whip me, baby. Whatever it takes to make you feel good. But let's not pretend you don't like it. You can bullshit them –' he jerked a thumb over his shoulder at the fans who still clustered at the locked door '– but not me. We're too close for that. Whipping people into a frenzy is why you got into it in the first place.'

Rachel pulled off her sunglasses and her eyes locked with Spector's. He had hit the nail on the head. She lived for the adulation, for the delirium she provoked, but she was dismayed to find that something she tried so hard to hide was so obvious. Frank could see it almost as clearly as Spector could, and that irked her.

Sy moved in to calm her down. His voice was soft and soothing. 'It's nothing to be ashamed of either – not for a second. It's a gift . . . and only a handful are given it. Many call but few are answered.'

Rachel laughed. The moment was defused. 'That's not quite how it's written in the Bible, Sy. I've been singing in Gospel choirs since I was six years old, so I know.'

'I'm quoting the entertainment industry Bible, honey. Don't fool with the blessing, Rachel. The magic is sustained by its use. You know that better than anyone.'

'Now *you*'re going to tell me about magic?' She shimmied her shoulders as if breaking free of him. She trotted ahead, making for the elevators. 'Give it a rest, will ya?'

Sy Spector threw up his hands as if ready to defend himself. 'I'm done. No more speeches. Not another word.' He smiled crookedly. 'I just know that you like to be reminded sometimes.'

Sy Spector glanced over at Frank Farmer as he spoke. His eyes telegraphed a clear message: You're good at your job, I'm good at mine . . .

CHAPTER FIFTEEN

Fireworks opened over the ocean, exploding in a blazing peacock's tail of red, green and shimmering gold. The glistening cinders cascaded toward the black water, carving bright streaks of fire in the night sky. The crowd on the balcony of Rachel Marron's penthouse suite oohed and aahed and clapped in appreciation.

The pre-concert nervousness that had infused Rachel and her staff had dissipated, replaced with the heady lightheartedness that always came after a show. Rachel had been on stage for a full two hours, singing her heart out, giving the audience more than their money's worth. By the end of the performance they were on their feet clapping and screaming, demanding more and more. Rachel did three encores before she could tear herself away from her worshiping fans.

The first-night party was in full swing and Rachel had as yet to make her entrance. Frank Farmer estimated that there were several hundred people scattered through the rooms of the suite. Some faces were famous and familiar; others were completely strange. And it was slightly unsettling to have so many people invading Rachel's living quarters.

There was a press of people around the two bars set up at either end of the room, and waiters threaded their way through the partygoers carrying large trays of canapés. Tony grabbed a handful of shrimps from one of the passing platters and stuffed them in his mouth. He was seated outside Rachel's bedroom, his bulk and his fierce look more than enough to keep intruders at bay.

The room continued to fill slowly. Al Thuringer had put uniformed security guards on the landing outside the suite, facing the elevators. As guests disembarked, their names were checked off against a master list, and then they were ushered through the arch of a metal detector.

From time to time the whole area was blasted with light as the TV crews and press photographers caught sight of some local Miami celebrity. All it took was for the press to spot the Dolphins' quarterback or a popular TV weatherman and the cameras opened up like artillery.

Among those streaming into the suite Frank Farmer saw someone from his past. Greg Portman was a tall, muscular man, about Frank's height but bulkier. He looked as if a single flex of his muscles would split the seams of his conservative suit.

'Hello, Farmer.'

Frank nodded. 'Portman.'

'Buy you a drink?' A waiter with a tray of champagne cruised by, and Portman neatly grabbed a glass as the man passed.

Frank held up his own glass. 'Orange juice.' He eyed Portman suspiciously. 'So, it's been a while . . .'

Frank Farmer and Greg Portman had been in the Secret Service at the same time. There had always been a subtle, insinuated rivalry between the two men – both had reputations for being among the best of their peculiar profession.

'You on the job?' Farmer asked.

Portman nodded. 'Technically I'm off duty, but the Governor might show up here later, so I thought I'd give it a light check.' He smiled wrily. 'Someone else is covering him right now.'

The Governor's reputation was well known in the Secret Service.

'Really?' said Frank. 'How old is she?'

Portman shrugged and laughed. 'Maybe eighteen. You working?'

Just then a roar went up from the partygoers as Rachel finally made her entrance. All heads were turned in her direction and there were applause and cheers.

'Thank you,' said Rachel. She posed, self-mockingly, as if allowing her devoted public to get a good look at her. 'Thank you all. Thank you. You're *so* right . . .'

Farmer nodded in Rachel's direction. 'My client,' he said.

Portman looked genuinely impressed. 'No kidding? I'd call that a step up from the President. She probably sings better too.'

'I want everyone to have a good time and drink as much of Ben Schiller's liquor as you like.' Rachel made her way through the crowd, laughing and blowing kisses.

Portman watched her act, appraising her critically, from a professional bodyguard's point of view. 'Why do I get the feeling she might be something of a handful?'

'If you only knew the half of it,' Frank grumbled.

'I heard you had to take someone out in New York.' Professional bodyguards had a gossip grapevine much like that of any other profession, and it had started buzzing the moment word of Frank's heroics got out.

'It was unavoidable,' said Frank, tight-lipped.

'It happens. I lost track of you after the Reagan thing.'

'Yeah,' said Frank curtly, making it clear that he did

147

not want to be reminded of the attempt on Ronald Reagan's life.

There was a pause while Frank's eyes scanned the room, alert, almost tense, as if expecting trouble.

'The Reagan thing wasn't your fault, Farmer. You weren't even there.'

'It was nobody's fault, Portman.'

The two men scrutinized the room, two sets of professional eyes. 'I got a call from New York. That guy you were covering – Klingman. He wanted me to come and work for him, take over where you left off. He said you'd recommended me.'

Frank smiled. 'Surprised?'

'A little.'

'I never doubted your skills.'

Portman laughed easily, good-natured. 'No, I guess not. The only things you doubted were my qualifications for the priesthood. You were always clear about that.'

'So? What happened with Klingman? The money was good.'

'I had to turn it down, Farmer. Something came up and I couldn't fit it in. I appreciate it, though. It's nice to be thought of.'

Portman noticed Rachel coming toward them. She was looking at him curiously. She took Frank's drink from his hand, sipped and grimaced.

'That's orange juice!' she said in disgust. She gave Greg Portman the once-over. She seemed to approve of what she saw. 'So, who are you?'

'I'm Greg Portman.'

'I take it you've met my bodyguard?'

'We used to work together. Frank and I go back a few years.'

Rachel seemed to grow more interested. 'Ah. Well, well, well. And what do you do now?'

Portman nodded. 'Same thing as Farmer.'

Rachel smiled. '*Two* samurai, eh?'

Frank and Portman eyed each other for a moment, like jealous rivals competing for the favors of the same woman.

'Frank was always more of a samurai than I was,' said Portman. 'He thinks more than I do. More cerebral, you know?'

'Tell me about it,' she said with a smirk. 'Are you working now?'

'Not right now.'

'Good. 'Cause I'm the only one in the room who needs protection.' She slipped her arm through his and pulled him into the crowd, shooting a glance over her shoulder at Frank as she went.

Frank watched as Rachel guided Portman out on to the balcony, snatching a glass of champagne from a waiter. She never took her eyes off Portman's face, leaning into him, their heads together whispering intimately. Portman said something and she laughed vivaciously. Then, for a brief moment, she turned her head and looked directly at Frank Farmer. Her look was petulant, defiant.

Frank turned away, not wanting to play her game. In that second there was a loud, sharp scream. He bolted for the balcony. Rachel and Portman were poised precariously halfway over the veranda railing. Frank's hand shot out and grabbed Rachel's wrist, tugging at her, but Portman regained his balance first and pulled Rachel back to safety.

'What happened?'

'Somebody tripped,' said Portman. 'It's okay.'

Rachel was shaken. 'Thank God I had a bodyguard here.' She stared down the twenty stories to the pool. 'It's a long way down, Frank. Portman saved my life.'

The front of her dress was stained with champagne. She led Portman past Frank and toward her bedroom. 'Maybe *someone* will keep an eye on me while I change.'

Frank and Portman locked eyes for a moment. Then Portman looked away and shrugged. It was plain that he felt bad for his fellow bodyguard.

There was nothing Frank could do about his client's pique. He made his way through the crowded room to the bar and got himself another orange juice. Behind the drinks table was a mirror, and reflected in the glass he could see Rachel leading Portman into her bedroom. He knew she knew he was watching her . . .

A stunningly beautiful young woman sidled up to him. She was tall and blonde, her skin glowing with the effects of a day in the sun. Her dress had a plunging neckline and she positioned herself so he could get a good view of her cleavage. Standing close to Frank, she seemed slightly unsteady on her feet, as if she might have had a touch too much to drink.

'I've been watching you all night from across the room,' she said, leering slightly.

'Really?'

'Uh-huh,' she said coyly.

'From where?'

She tossed her long blonde locks. 'From over there.'

'Well, why don't you go back there and keep watching?' He turned on his heel and walked back outside.

Rachel and Portman were kissing, locked in a clinch, his hands exploring her body, sliding up under the silk of her dress. Suddenly she realized what she was doing and pulled back, catching herself.

'I'm not doing this . . .' she murmured.

Portman held her close. 'I think you are.'

She shook off his embrace, stepping away from him quickly. 'I said I was grateful. Thank you and good night.' She started toward the door.   'Please go now,' she said coolly.

Portman reached for her arm, wanting to pull her back to him and toward the wide, king-size bed. Rachel avoided his grasp and opened the door. Tony, still at his post, looked up as the door swung open.

'You okay, Rachel?'

'Mr Portman was just leaving us, Tony.'

Portman hesitated a moment, then smiled at Rachel and her giant assistant. He leaned forward and gave Rachel a peck on the cheek, then slipped by them and back into the party. Rachel briefly scanned the crowd, looking for Frank, but did not see him. She stepped back into her room and closed the door. Standing on the sideboard was a collection of bottles. She grabbed the one closest – Scotch – twisted off the cap and drank deep.

There was no one on the balcony now and Frank was glad of that. He leaned against the railing and gazed out to sea, looking at the moonlight as it reflected off the ocean and listening to the steady beat of the surf. It was peaceful and quiet there, a relief after the heat and confusion of the party going on inside.

He thought he was alone, but then he noticed a figure forty feet away on the balcony of the suite next door. It was Mark Katz, the boy he had encountered with Al Thuringer earlier that day. Frank smiled over at the kid.

'Go to sleep,' said Farmer.

Frank turned to stare at the ocean again. Music was drifting out from the party. 'What Becomes of the Broken-hearted . . .' The sound was slow and sweet and it seemed a long way away. For a moment everything around him seemed far off. There was only the moon and the ocean. For the moment his guard was down.

CHAPTER SIXTEEN

Rachel surfaced around noon the next day, haggard and hung-over. She was dressed in a loose smock, and her bloodshot eyes were hidden behind dark glasses. Her pounding headache was exacerbated by the noise of the howling vacuum cleaner that a maid was running over the carpet.

'Turn that off!' she snapped.

'But –'

'I said turn it off!'

The howl of the electric motor died away, and the maid scurried into another room to escape the wrath of the star. Rachel walked down the hallway to the kitchen of the suite and found Frank seated at the table, eating his lunch. Another place had been laid, set with breakfast. She slumped into the chair, as if the walk to the kitchen had required immense effort. Examining the eggs and toast on her plate with distaste, she picked up a mug of coffee and drank. Frank glanced at her, then quickly turned his attention to his sandwich.

'What the hell are you looking at?' Rachel's voice was strained and her tone nasty. 'You probably never had a heavy night in your whole goddamn disciplined life.'

Frank continued to chew.

'You know, Farmer, you're a self-righteous son of a bitch!'

Frank found himself smiling at her. The smirk pushed Rachel to further heights of fury. 'Don't laugh at me, goddammit!' she shouted. 'And don't you *dare* judge me.'

Frank put down his sandwich. 'Give me a break, will ya? I didn't tell you to fuck everybody in the whole hotel.'

'Farmer –' Rachel stopped. Tony was standing in the doorway.

'Uh, Frank. Phone call for you . . .'

He nodded and picked up the telephone extension in the kitchen.

'Frank! Ray Court here.'

'How you doing, Ray?' Farmer wondered how the Secret Service agent had managed to track him down. It was probably very simple. Court had probably called Rachel Marron's office in Los Angeles and they had told him . . . More bad security.

'Can't complain,' said Court. 'Listen, we're getting a match on the glue the psycho used on the note. It was part of a batch shipped to LA. So he's a local crazy.'

'That narrows it down to about two million nuts,' said Frank.

'Nah, don't worry about it. We're getting to him. We're gonna nail this fucker.'

'Yeah, well, don't take too long.'

Ray Court chuckled. 'Hey, Frank . . .'

'Yeah?'

'It's good money, isn't it?'

''Bye, Ray,' said Frank putting down the phone. He turned back to Rachel. 'Good news. It turns out –'

'I don't give a shit,' she said nastily. Then she stood up abruptly and ran down the hall, slamming the bedroom door behind her.

Frank sighed and decided to take a walk on the beach.

He returned to the suite an hour or two later. As he stepped out of the elevator, he was surprised to see that the uniformed hotel security guard was not at his post outside the front door of the penthouse.

Frank let himself in with his key and looked around the apartment quickly. Nothing had been disturbed, but there was no sign of Rachel or Tony either.

Bill Devaney emerged from the balcony.

'Where is she?' Frank demanded. 'Where's Tony?'

'I don't know,' said Devaney. 'I thought she was with you.'

'Dammit!' Frank snatched up the phone, angrily punching a number. 'Thuringer, this is Farmer. Where the hell is she? What do you mean you don't know? And where the hell is your man on the door?' Frank listened a moment. 'Well, get someone up here right now.'

Frank slammed down the phone. 'He doesn't know where she is. But he did say that she dismissed the guard on the door.'

Devaney shook his head. 'Frank, I'm sorry . . .'

Frank started toward the door.

'Where are you going?'

'I'm going to go find her.'

But there was no need. There was laughter on the other side of the door and the sound of a key being inserted in the lock. Frank pulled the door open. Rachel and Tony were standing there, their arms filled with boxes and bags. They were in high spirits, all signs of her hang-over having vanished. She ignored Frank.

'Hello, Devaney.' Rachel dumped her packages on an armchair and went to the bar to make a drink for herself. 'Did Fletcher call?'

'Rachel, where the hell have you been?' Devaney allowed his anger to show.

'I asked you if my son called.'

'No, he didn't, and where the hell have you been?'

'Tony and I went over to Bal Harbor.' She winked at Tony. 'Did a little shopping. No crime in that, right?'

'We were worried,' said Devaney. He was talking to her but looking at Frank. 'You know you're not supposed to do that.'

'C'mon, Bill . . . I'm a big girl. I can take care of myself, you know that.'

'No, you can't,' said Frank quietly.

Rachel wheeled around. 'Don't talk to me like that, Farmer. You work here. Do you understand that? You work for me. I'm the boss.'

'Rachel . . .' Devaney put out a hand to restrain her. Frank turned and started for the door again. 'Farmer, where are you going?' Devaney was terrified that he was going to walk out of the suite and keep on going, leaving him to deal with the security mess.

'I'm going to go check the route. As usual.'

Seething with tension and rage, Frank made his way down to the kitchen and ballroom, examining the course that Rachel would travel later that night as she made her way on stage for the second of her sold-out shows.

The kitchen was its usual riotous clatter and kitchen workers scurried out of his way as he strode through. One look at his face was enough to tell anybody that Frank Farmer was not to be bothered that afternoon.

The corridor that led to the stage was empty, and the store rooms that led off the hallway were supposed to be kept locked during the time that Rachel was in the hotel. He checked the locks and found that all but one of them was secure.

Frank flicked on the light and saw that the room

was stacked high with empty wooden crates. Beyond them, sitting in the shadows, was a man. He was huge and dark, his black hair an unruly mop of curls. Farmer figured him to be a Cuban, but he didn't wear the white uniform of the kitchen staff. The man didn't bat an eye when he saw Frank.

'Who the hell are you?' Farmer demanded. 'What are you doing here?'

The Cuban hardly moved a muscle. 'Is none of your fuckin' business,' he said, his accent heavy with disdain and danger.

Frank held the door open. 'Out. Move it.'

The enormous man lumbered to his feet, towering over Frank. 'Hey, shove it up your ass, motherfucker.'

Frank had been jerked around too much that day to care how much he hurt the man. He came in low and hard, putting all his weight behind two fast blows to the gut. The punches staggered the big Cuban, who toppled forward, his arms encircling Farmer, trying to drag him down. Farmer slid out of the grasp and kicked, spearing the man in the chest, throwing him into the pile of crates and on into the concrete wall.

The Cuban hit the cement hard, the back of his head slapping forcefully. He shook off the shock and seized a mop, swinging the wooden shaft like a baseball bat. Frank stepped in and under the wide arc of the pole and smashed the Cuban in the chest and jaw, his fists a blur. The punches thudded home, rocking the man. Then Frank smashed both the Cuban's ears simultaneously and the man felt an explosion of pain deep in the center of his skull.

He sank to his knees on the cold floor, stunned. Frank was in the mood to inflict a little more pain on his fallen foe, but before he could kick the Cuban into a bleeding heap at his feet he heard a scream.

'Stop! Please! Don't hurt him! Please stop!' A woman in a chambermaid's uniform was hurrying toward them, her purse clutched to her chest. Tears were streaming from her eyes. 'Stop!'

'Who the hell is he?' asked Frank fiercely.

'He is my husband, mister. Don't hurt him. He don't do nothing. He just waiting here to pick me up, give me a ride home.' The woman fell to the concrete and threw her arms around her husband. 'Ohh,' she groaned. 'Luis, *pobrecito*.'

Breathing hard, Frank Farmer leaned back against the wall, disgusted with himself.

'I'm sorry,' he said.

The chambermaid raised her tear-stained face to look up at Frank, uncomprehending. 'Why you do this thing?'

'I'm sorry . . . I don't know.' Frank walked away quickly, rubbing his hand through his hair, trying to collect himself. He shoved open the stage door and stared out into the bright, hot light of a Florida afternoon. The first thing he saw was the marquee over the theater. The words seemed to taunt him.

RACHEL MARRON. TONITE. BENEFIT CONCERT. 8PM.

He knew it was time to get out.

CHAPTER SEVENTEEN

Rachel sat at her dressing table, applying the make-up she would wear on stage. Having put Farmer in his place, she felt pretty good, and she could sense herself getting pumped up for the performance. Humming to herself, she started on her hair. The phone rang and she smiled at herself in the mirror. It was her private line, a number that did not have to go through the hotel switchboard – a select few had this number. She knew who this was going to be.

She picked up the receiver. 'Fletcher?'

There was no response.

'Baby, is that you? It's Mommy, honey.'

The voice was eerily distorted, cold and menacing. 'Guess again, whore! Fuck you and fuck Miami. I'm coming for you. I know where you are and I'm coming for you.'

'Oh, my God!' Rachel slammed down the phone and dashed from the room. She flew into the living room and threw herself into Bill Devaney's arms.

She could barely speak through her sobs. 'It was . . . It was . . .'

'What? What's the matter, baby?'

'*Him*. He was on the phone.'

'Jesus! How did he –?'

'Oh, my God, Bill, he threatened to kill me. He called me names.'

Bill Devaney led her back to the bedroom. 'Lie down, baby. Don't answer the phone. I'll get Farmer.'

★

Striding into the hotel room, Frank answered the page that Devaney put out through Thuringer. His mind was made up.

'I'm through,' he said. 'I'll get you back to Los Angeles and that's it. The guy with Fletcher can cover until you can get a replacement.'

Devaney hastily stubbed out his cigarette and jumped to his feet. 'She got another call while you were downstairs. She answered it herself. It was *him*, Frank. Same guy.'

'I don't care,' said Frank shortly.

'Farmer, it really shook her up. She thought it was going to be Fletcher calling from LA. I think she'll be reasonable from now on.'

Frank Farmer shrugged.

Devaney could tell that he meant what he said. He really *was* through.

Frank opened the door leading out to the balcony. 'The concert? I assume it's still on.'

Devaney nodded. 'You can't cancel these things at the last minute. Unfortunately.'

'Call me when she's ready to go down.' Frank stepped outside and closed the glass door behind him.

He took a deep breath of the sweet ocean air and rested his elbows on the railings, looking out to sea. A yacht was gliding past the hotel, just a few hundred yards offshore, its lights gleaming in the dusk. Frank had told Fletcher that he hated boats, but right then he wished he was on board that yacht, sailing solo for some distant port. He could imagine the sounds – the luff of the sails as they fell off the wind and the clean slice of the bow through the fat waves.

He heard the door open behind him and he glanced over his shoulder. Rachel was dressed in her costume. Her hair was brushed and she was wearing her stage make-up – the performance armor that protected her when she was before her audience. But somehow, this time, her disguise didn't work. The air of supreme confidence wasn't there. She held a cigarette in her hand, the wind blowing across the tip, making it glow orange. He had never seen her smoke before.

'Farmer,' she said quietly, 'I want you to know that nothing that's happened between us matters ... I understand now. You're going to have to believe me because I'm not going to beg.'

She took a long drag on the cigarette and exhaled. As if there were a loop of tape in her brain, she replayed the caller's words in her mind over and over again, hearing the hate.

'It wasn't what he said. It was the way he said it. He was so ...' Her voice cracked and her shoulders drooped and she seemed to wilt for a moment. Then she composed herself, squaring her shoulders and clearing her throat.

'I need you ... I'm afraid ... and I hate it. I hate my fear.'

Frank nodded. This was the problem in a nutshell. Rachel Marron could not stand to be weak and she could not tolerate needing another person to keep her alive. She had come as far as she had on her own, building her stardom with grit and determination. Now she had to rely on someone else for the most visceral, basic need of all.

'Please protect me. Protect Fletcher. If anything happened to him, I don't know –' Tears sprang into her eyes and slipped down her cheeks, carving wet tracks in her elaborate make-up. She wiped the tears away.

'I can't protect you like this,' said Frank. He waved at the suite as if conjuring up the crowds and confusion of the night before. 'It's impossible. The odds are on his side.'

'I'll do whatever you say.'

This was the first time Frank had ever heard Rachel say that. He studied her for a moment, then looked back out over the ocean. The yacht was rounding the point, slipping out of view. 'I want to take you away for a while.'

'When?'

'Immediately. Tomorrow.'

'But I have the Oscars coming up on the –'

Frank shot her a look, grimacing.

She smiled and shrugged. 'I'm sorry, I'm sorry . . . Where are we going?'

'Somewhere people don't know about.'

She nodded.

'No Spector or Devaney or Tony.' He studied her face, looking for any hesitation on her part. He saw only acceptance.

'And if you cross me up this time, I'll kill you myself. Understood?'

Rachel smiled weakly but with obvious relief. 'Understood,' she said.

CHAPTER EIGHTEEN

They drove out of Los Angeles – Nicki, Rachel, Fletcher, Henry and Farmer packed into a perfectly ordinary Dodge Minivan, heading north of Interstate Five. It was a long two-day drive to central Oregon, but it was, to Frank's mind, a better way of getting there than flying. Most of the news organizations and gossip columnists had tipsters at the Los Angeles airport who would pass along the information that Rachel Marron and family, *and* an unidentified male, had boarded a plane for Portland, Oregon.

They drove all day, up through the central valley, an anonymous van in the middle of a steady stream of traffic. Fletcher sat up front with Frank, staring out the window. He watched the fields and the small towns and the truck stops slip by as if he had never seen anything so amazing in his life. Frank figured that was a normal reaction – everyday life looked a little different to someone used to seeing the world from a Bel Air mansion or from the back of a limousine.

In the rear of the van Rachel, Nicki and Henry sang. They worked their way through Gospel, Motown and fifties oldies: Sam Cook, Jackie Wilson, Chuck Berry, LaVern Baker, Solomon Burke. The two sisters, who seemed to know every word of every verse of every song ever written, sang jazzy harmony, while Henry filled in with a pretty fair baritone. Frank glanced in the mirror from time to time, catching Rachel's eye, and felt that he had made the right decision. For the first time since he'd met her, she seemed to be happy.

By nightfall they were in northern California and had checked into a nondescript motel on Route 97, just outside a town with the unlovely name of Weed. It was a long way from the Presidential Suite at the Fontainebleau Hotel, but Rachel, Nicki and Fletcher were in high spirits. It was a relief, for once, to be completely ordinary, to be free of the trappings of celebrity. They ate at the local Kentucky Fried Chicken as if the food were a gourmet delight served at Morton's or Spago.

They drove for most of the next day, through the majestic scenery around Klamath Falls, Crater Lake and the Fremont National Forest. It was spring in the rest of the country, high summer already in Florida, but up here in the mountains winter still lingered, snow lying in patches on the slowly thawing ground and as thick white mantles in the trees of the rolling forest country. They drove through the little towns on Route 97 – Chemult, Crescent, Gilchrist, La Pine, Sunriver – and on to their destination.

The little town of Bend, Oregon, sits on the Deschutes River, a few miles outside the Deschutes National Forest and hard by the spine of mountains called the Cascades, the northern branch of the Rockies, which extend clear into Canada. It is as peaceful and as beautiful a spot as you could hope to find anywhere; it is also remote and secure, the kind of place where everybody knows everybody else, where a stranger will be noticed.

Bend was also Frank Farmer's hometown. His father, Herb, was one of the leading citizens of the county, having been chief of police there for twenty-five years.

Frank drove through the town and out toward Pilot

Butte Lake and his family home. The large, old, rambling two-story house sat at the top of a slight rise, bordered on three sides by thick, silent pine woods. Sloping down from the house was a broad expanse of lawn, still encrusted with snow all the way to the lakeshore. Frank saw that beyond the Farmer dock and boathouse, the lake was free of ice.

A wire-haired terrier charged out of the house at their approach, barking and skittering on the asphalt drive. A man in his sixties emerged and stood on the porch watching the van pull into the turn-around in front of the house. Herb Farmer was a lean, tan, fit-looking man, dressed in a plaid shirt, faded old jeans and scuffed cowboy boots. His eyes were a bright, curious blue. His hair was white. Looking at him, it was easy to see how his son would age.

Frank got out of the van and eyed his father. Both men were delighted to be reunited after three years' separation, but neither of them betrayed an ounce of emotion. It was as if Frank had just returned from a quick trip into town to pick up some odds and ends at the grocery store. The little dog was not so low-key. He capered and jumped, licking Frank's hand.

'Lake's a little low,' said Frank.

'It'll fill up soon enough when the thaw comes.' Farmer senior cocked his square chin at the passengers in the van. 'They all in trouble?'

Frank slid his hands into the back pockets of his jeans. 'Only one,' he said.

Frank had no doubt what Fletcher wanted to do first. The little fishing skiff that Herb Farmer kept on the lake didn't have much more power than Fletcher's radio-remote-controlled model boat, but it had one huge advantage in Fletcher's eyes: it was an honest-to-

God boat, one that you could get in and steer. He looked at the trim little craft, wide-eyed, as if gazing at the *Queen Mary*.

Rachel, Frank and Fletcher, along with the gamboling terrier, Sparky, made their way down to the dock while Nicki and Henry brought in the luggage and got started with the unpacking. Fletcher and Sparky had already become fast friends, running and cavorting in the snow while Frank checked the fuel tank. There was plenty in the can, so he started to squeeze the bulb pump to put some gasoline in the engine to prime it. Rachel stood on the dock watching her boy and the dog.

'That little dog is going to protect us?' she asked sceptically.

'He's a trained noise-maker.'

'Terrific,' she said, unconvinced.

'Big dogs are okay sometimes,' said Frank. 'But they don't always know who they're eating. Hey, Fletcher!'

'Yeah?' He was rolling in the snow, giggling, while Sparky attempted to lick his face.

'Time to get under way.'

'Great.'

Frank helped Rachel and the boy into the boat. She sat in the bow and snuggled in her down coat.

'It'll be cold out there.' She looked out at the lake and shivered.

'We won't be out long. The sun's going down. This is just a get-acquainted cruise.'

'Get acquainted with what?'

'With the boat. Fletcher, grab the starter handle and give it a yank.' Frank opened the fuel cock and advanced the spark, and Fletcher grabbed the cord with both hands and pulled. The engine sputtered, coughed and kicked but did not catch. Fletcher tumbled back in the boat.

'Fletcher's not much of a swimmer,' said Rachel nervously.

'Well, then, he'd better stay in the boat.' Farmer cast off the spring line and then dug a bright-orange Mae West life jacket from the locker in the bow. 'C'mon, Fletcher, put one of these things on.'

'Aww, do I have to?'

'Yes.'

The kid slipped into the giant vest and Frank laced it tight. 'Okay, try that engine again.'

Fletcher yanked mightily and this time the engine burst into life. 'I did it!' he yelped in delight.

'Well, then, take the control and steer us out.'

Fletcher sat in the stern, the tiller under his thin little arm, his hand on the throttle, and, as serious as a pilot on the bridge of a supertanker, he took the little craft into the lake. Sparky stood tense as sprung steel on the dock, whimpering as they sailed away. For a moment he feinted toward the water, as if to jump in and swim after them in hot pursuit.

The trip around Pilot Butte Lake was like a tour through Frank Farmer's boyhood. He showed them where he had spent lazy summer days fishing for perch, the coves where wall-eyed pike and wide-mouth bass could be taken in the fall and featureless places in the middle of the water where he and his father had cut holes in the frozen lake and built their ice fishing houses.

Frank showed them the mysterious places of his youth. There was the inlet where the water was always a little colder than the rest of the lake because an underwater spring fed into it, a vent so deep that generations of boys had tried to dive down far enough to find it but no one had ever succeeded.

'Really?' gasped Fletcher.

'Still down there if you want to try and find it.'

The boy peered into the black water and shivered at the thought of the spring down there in the dark. 'No, thanks.'

'Smart kid,' Rachel observed.

Fletcher was enchanted by the stories, but the boat captivated him. Gradually, he increased the speed of the vessel, bringing it up to top speed, getting all the power he could out of the forty-horse-power engine. He locked the throttle in place and raised his arms in a 'Look, Ma, no hands' gesture.

They cruised around the water until the sun was low in the sky and the shadows of the pine trees lengthened across the lake. A mist was rising.

'Okay, Fletcher,' Frank called into the wind. 'Time to head in.'

Obediently, the little boy leaned on the tiller, taking the boat into a long, controlled curve, heading back for the shore. Henry and Sparky were waiting for them on the dock.

'C'mon, Fletcher,' said Rachel, 'let's go in the house. I'm freezing.' Together mother and son clambered out of the boat and started up toward the house.

'You get in the boat, Henry,' ordered Frank. 'I want you to see how it gets put to bed.'

Frank ran the skiff slowly over to the boathouse and killed the engine before cruising through the open lake-side mouth of the building. The boat bumped and rocked against the pier and Frank tied up.

'I hate to keep on bringing up a sore subject . . .'

'What? What did I do?'

Frank smiled. 'Nothing. We have to talk about bombs.'

'Again with the bombs.'

'A boat is very easy to booby-trap. Much easier than

168

a car, but traps in boats are a lot easier to spot. They can be placed only in three places. Here.' He tapped the red gas can. 'Here.' He pointed to the ignition spark control. 'And here.' He pulled open the top of the outboard. 'The electrodes get attached to the shaft housing and when the engine hits a certain number of revs, the thing blows.'

Henry nodded. 'I get it.'

'I don't want you or Fletcher going out in it until you've checked it over. You see anything other than what you see now, you get away fast.'

Henry peered into the mechanism as if memorizing it. 'Got it.'

'Remember, check it out. Every time.'

'Right,' said Henry. 'Every time.'

Frank found Rachel looking at a wall of photographs, following the Farmer family history in pictures. There was Frank as a ten-year-old baseball player, then a younger Herb who sported a stiff buzz crew-cut. There was a photograph of Herb in full police uniform being given a civic award by the mayor of Bend. There was a duplicate of the picture she had seen in Frank's basement, a young Frank as a football wide receiver. In the center of all the pictures, occupying the place of honor, was a photo of Herb and Katherine Farmer, all dressed up, their son introducing his parents to President Jimmy Carter.

On the outer edge of the gallery Rachel noticed a photo of a smiling Henry Kissinger talking to a knot of female reporters. Standing shoulder to shoulder with him were Frank and Portman. The camera had captured Kissinger's well-known eye for the ladies, freezing him in the middle of a mild bout of flirtation. Portman was also smiling, bantering with the women.

Frank, however, was in his familiar pose, alert, unsmiling, wary and watchful. Rachel examined the two men for a second or two.

'Portman sometimes had trouble remembering just what his job was.'

'Hey, Frank?' his father called from the kitchen.

'Dad?'

'Set the table. Supper's almost ready.'

He smiled at Rachel. 'His master's voice . . .'

Rachel was drawn into the kitchen by the smell of roasting chicken. Herb Farmer had long ago gotten used to fixing his own simple meals and, set in his ways, he had refused Nicki's offer of a helping hand. He would rather do all the cooking himself. Rachel, drink in hand, stood watching as he chopped vegetables for a salad, sure and practiced, methodical, like his son. The low-ceilinged kitchen was as neatly organized as the bridge of a ship.

'Katherine had this place organized just the way she wanted it,' he said, not looking up from the chopping block.

'Katherine?'

'Frank's momma,' he said matter-of-factly. 'My wife.'

'Oh,' she said. 'I didn't know she –'

'It was a long time ago.' Herb smiled a crooked smile. 'Frank tells me you're a singer of some sort.'

Rachel laughed. 'Of some sort . . . That's right.' Frank looked a little embarrassed.

'I didn't mean – Well, I guess you must be pretty famous, but I'm afraid we're a little out of touch here. I'm sorry.'

'Don't worry about it.'

'You must be very successful to need Frank.'

'Too successful, I guess.' She gazed out the window.

The sun was below the treeline now and the lake was a vast tract of inky black. 'It's so quiet here. Peaceful.'

Herb sighed. 'Yep. It's a good place. Frank came back here and stayed six months after the Reagan thing.'

Rachel remembered the 'Reagan thing'. It had been a gray day in March, and she had been a nobody then. She was on the road with a band someplace, but it was an off day, a Monday, a day to recover from the weekend gig at some dive on Route 57 south of Chicago. All she had planned to do that night was watch the Academy Awards and dream of being there one day herself. Reagan had been shot in Washington in the afternoon and they had postponed the Oscars . . .

'Frank wasn't there the day he was shot. He never got over that.' Herb quickly diced some carrots. ''Course, he should have been there – he was in the presidential detail.'

'Where was he?'

'He was here,' said Herb. 'We buried Katherine that day.' He slipped on some oven mitts, opened the stove and took out a steaming Pyrex bowl of golden scalloped potatoes. 'Put these on the table,' he said, 'and call the others.'

Because of the long drive and the brief, brisk boat trip on the lake everybody at the table was hungry. Fletcher had torn enthusiastically into his chicken, his face covered with breadcrumbs and gravy. Now he was demolishing a bowl of ice cream with a generous ration of chocolate sauce.

Herb Farmer, unused to having company at dinner, drank wine and found himself growing loquacious. In the manner of parents everywhere, he delighted in regaling his son's friends with embarrassing tales of Frank's childhood.

'. . . And to this day I never hit him. Never, ever. To this day.' He looked to Frank for confirmation. 'That's true, isn't it?'

Frank nodded. 'Absolutely,' he said.

'That's very unusual for my people,' Herb continued. 'So what happens? When he's ten years old, he complains about it. Can you believe that?'

'Oh, for Chrissake!' Frank exploded in laughter. 'I'm going to tell them about the time you stripped in court.'

'You did what?' shrieked Nicki.

'I don't care if you tell them that. I'm *proud* of that, dammit.'

Frank stood up and started clearing the table.

'Why did you want your dad to hit you, Frank? Seems kinda crazy to me.' Fletcher looked puzzled.

'You said a mouthful, sonny. I'll tell you. He's just ten years old and he's just started playing tackle football. He comes to me and he tells me he's afraid of getting hit, right? And he thinks it's because I never hit him. "Why don't you ever hit me?" he says to me.'

'If you're lucky, maybe he'll tell you about my first jockstrap,' Frank called from the kitchen. He peered out the window at the lake.

'He got over it,' he could hear his father continuing. 'He turned into a helluva wide receiver. He couldn't stand being afraid. When he found something that scared him he'd just do it until the fear went away.' Herb finished his wine and pushed back his chair. 'His mother was the same way . . .'

He stood, walked to a cabinet, opened it, pulled out a chessboard and placed it on the dining table. The pieces were not in their orderly ranks. This was a game in progress. Herb Farmer leaned over and blew on the board as if it were a birthday cake, sending up a small blue cloud of dust.

'Come on, son. You can run but you can't hide.'

Frank appeared from the kitchen and sat down. 'Whose move was it?'

'Yours, if memory serves.'

Frank studied the chessmen, trying to remember what his strategy had been when the game commenced. 'Let's see . . .'

'How long has this game been going on?' asked Rachel, her chin cupped in her hand. She draped her other arm across Fletcher's thin shoulders.

'Three years,' said Frank.

'He had me on the run there, the first year and a half. Now things are changing, going my way.'

Frank touched the bishop, then the rook, uncertain about his move. He turned to Fletcher. 'What do you think?'

'Knight to king four,' said Fletcher.

Frank read the gambit, playing it out in his mind. 'Good move.'

Herb stared hard at the child.

'City kid,' explained Frank.

By nine o'clock that evening Rachel and Nicki were in their rooms, Fletcher was asleep in front of the fire and Herb was dozing at his side. Frank was making his final rounds of the night, checking windows and rattling door knobs, reminding himself that they were locked. Sparky trotted at his heels.

From within the darkened house he gazed out at the lake. The water was invisible, the whole lake was shrouded in mist. The only sign that it was there at all was the sound of the water gently lapping against the dock. Using the fog as cover, an intruder could probably walk unseen up to the door of the house, but Sparky would have drawn a bead on him well before that. Frank felt secure.

A light went on in the kitchen and Frank turned to see Nicki filling a glass of water at the sink.

'Still up?' he asked with a smile. 'It's late – almost nine fifteen.'

She answered his smile. 'The middle of the night. What are you doing?'

'Just locking up.'

'You're very thorough.'

'All part of the job.'

Nicki sipped her water. 'And Rachel? She part of the job too?'

Frank glanced at her sharply. 'Give me a break, Nicki. Please.'

'Come on, Frank. One minute she's got magnetic hands, the next she hates you. I can't figure out what it is *now*.' She had raised her voice slightly and Herb stirred in his sleep.

Frank walked into the kitchen and closed the door. 'You always follow all her moves this closely?'

Nicki smiled. 'It's a living.'

'No, it isn't,' he said pointedly.

'You think my life is pretty sick, don't you?'

Frank looked away. 'No.'

'You must,' she insisted. '*I* do.'

'Then why don't you change it? Do something about it.'

'Is it that easy?' She put her hands on his shoulders and pulled him close, kissing him warmly. He kissed back for a moment, then pulled away.

'You're a lovely woman,' he said.

Nicki's voice had a hard, sharp edge. 'But you don't want me.'

Frank didn't have to answer. His look told her all she needed to know. Nicki's face fell, pierced by the sudden pain of rejection. She felt hot anger, driven by embarrassment and his rebuff, rising within her. 'I'm surprised. Thorough fellow like you . . . Why stop at one sister when you can fuck them both?'

'I make my mistakes,' said Frank, 'but I live with them.'

'But you didn't say no to the boss.' She started to turn away, but his hands were on her, holding her close, refusing to let her go. Their faces were close and he spoke forcefully.

'No, don't leave, Nicki. Don't leave me with that. Tell me about it.'

'Tell what? She's the star. I'm not. End of story.'

'No,' protested Frank. 'Tell me how long you've been second. Tell me how she has a child and you don't. Tell me something. But don't turn away and try to stick it on me. Take responsibility for your life.'

Nicki twisted in his grasp, trying to break away. He held her tight, turning her face back to confront him. 'I don't need this from you,' she said.

'Maybe *I* need it.' He spoke through clenched teeth. 'I'm fed up with people telling me they have no control over their lives. If you hate your life so much, turn it around. You're not trapped. You can go any time you want.'

Tears appeared in the corner of Nicki's brown eyes. 'It's not that simple.'

'Yes, it is. You can walk out of that fucking door any time you want. I'll unlock it for you.'

'Let me go.' Nicki struggled in his arms and he stepped back, allowing her to go free.

'Okay,' he said. 'It's really none of my business.'

CHAPTER NINETEEN

The bright morning sun was reflected on the crisp snow, shimmering and intensifying the dazzling radiance. Frank and Herb walked along the lake shoreline. They stopped from time to time to examine tracks and spoor in the snow and mud. They found that the property had been visited in the night by racoon and deer and a variety of wading waterfowl.

Frank paused a moment and looked out at the lake, shading his eyes against the sun.

'Nice here, isn't it?' asked Herb.

'Sure is.'

'Ever considered coming home for good?'

'Sure. All the time.'

'And will you?'

'Yes. But not yet.'

From the house they could hear the clink of dishes and glassware being cleared from the breakfast table. The utensils clattered into the sink. Nicki and Rachel were doing the dishes together, singing Gospel songs as they worked.

'I've never heard church music in the middle of the week before,' observed Herb.

But Frank wasn't listening. He had noticed another set of tracks in the snow, the heavy prints of a predator. They were the imprints of thick-soled snow boots leading into the tree line at the edge of the property.

'Where's Fletcher?'

At that moment the outboard motor coughed into

life. Frank's head snapped toward the boathouse. Henry appeared at the back door.

'Frank!' he shouted frantically. 'I haven't –'

Frank was off and running, pounding across the lawn, dashing for the dock. Fletcher had pulled the skiff out of the boathouse and was slowly chugging along, parallel to the pier.

'Fletcher! Fletcher!' The little boy, intent on piloting the boat, did not look up to see Frank running frantically for the dock, and he couldn't hear him over the drone of the motor.

The boards of the dock rattled and shook as Frank sprinted its length. He reached the end just as the boat rounded the farthest point of the pier.

Frank didn't hesitate. He dove directly for the rear of the boat, knocking Fletcher from his perch in the stern, both of them falling into the frigid water.

Rachel was on the porch, staring, her heart pounding in her chest. The instant they hit the water she screamed.

'No! He can't swim!'

Fletcher was crying in Frank's arms, shocked and scared at finding himself thrown into the water so suddenly. Frank hooked his left arm under the boy's shoulders and swam with his right hand toward the shore. The boat was still chugging out into the lake, picking up speed.

Rachel was livid with anger building toward hysteria. 'Fletcher, baby. Are you all right? Baby? Speak to me!'

Henry fell flat on the dock and helped haul the two dripping bodies out of the water. Fletcher was coughing and spluttering, trembling in his sodden jacket. Henry stripped it off and quickly wrapped the frail child in his huge down coat.

'You're all right, aren't you, Fletcher?'

The little boy managed to nod.

Frank sat on the end of the dock, breathing hard, his mind reeling.

'What the hell are you doing? You out of your mind?' Rachel screamed. 'You're crazy! You could have drowned him!'

Frank shook his head. 'I'm sorry. I got careless.'

Henry felt that he shared the blame. 'Frank, I'm sorry. I should have . . .'

'It's okay, Henry,' said Frank wearily.

'You all right now, son?' It was not clear which person Herb was talking to.

Henry looked out on the lake. The boat was about five hundred yards away, still plowing through the water, outbound. 'How do we get the boat back?'

Then the boat exploded. There was a puff of gray smoke, followed almost instantaneously by the detonation of explosives. The boat vanished, replaced by a burning spot on the water, thick black sooty smoke staining the bright blue sky.

Nicki and Rachel screamed. Frank turned his back on the burning boat and held out his hand, palm down. His hand was trembling.

Frank and Henry went over the van in meticulous detail, but they could not figure out how it had been disabled. The same applied to Herb's beat-up pick-up. Both cars were absolutely dead.

Herb came out of the house, walking quickly. 'Frank,' he said urgently. 'The phone line has been cut. It could be anywhere between here and town.'

Frank nodded, as if he expected this development. 'And both cars are dead. And I can't figure out how it was done.'

Frank and Herb exchanged worried looks. 'Who could know we're here? This place has nothing to do with her. How could he have traced us up here?'

'Maybe it's not about her. Maybe it has something to do with you.'

Frank shook his head. 'If someone wanted me, he would have attacked head-on, and it would have happened a long time ago.' He thought a moment. 'We have to get them out of here.'

'How?'

'We walk.'

'Son, it's fourteen miles to the main road. Thirty miles to town.'

'Yeah, I know.'

Herb looked at the sky. 'The sun will have set before you get to the highway. You can't walk them out at night. He could be waiting out there.'

Frank nodded. 'You're right. We'll button down tonight and walk out at first light.'

At first the night seemed silent with the mute hush of peaceful darkness, but as Frank concentrated on listening the gloom became alive with noise. The wind blew through the pines; there was the cry of a night bird. The old house creaked and settled. From the basement came the low, airy roar as the furnace switched on. The condenser in the refrigerator whirred . . .

Frank had been sitting in the middle of the living room, his gun in his lap, waiting for dawn. Mentally he ran through the positions of the people in the house. Henry was in his room; Nicki was in hers; Fletcher was with Rachel; Herb was right across the hall; Sparky was stationed on the upstairs landing.

Then there came a new sound. It was in the kitchen, a low, sad sobbing. Nicki . . .

She was sitting with her head in her hands, an open bottle of Bourbon at her elbow, an empty glass in front of her. She turned her tear-streaked face to Frank when he walked in, gun in hand.

'I was an idiot last night,' she said softly.

He touched her shoulder, as if to reassure her.

'What do you think about today, Frank?' she asked.

'I think . . .' he said gently. 'I think this is no maniac. I think he knows what he's doing.'

There was a long, long silence between them, broken only by Nicki's sobs. Finally, she dried her eyes and spoke. 'You're right. He does.'

'Tell me about it.'

She stared at the empty glass for a moment, then reached for the Bourbon bottle. He closed his hand over hers and held the liquor bottle in place.

'Who is it, Nicki?' His voice was tense, urgent. 'Tell me, and I can stop him.'

'He almost got Fletcher today . . .'

His voice tightened. 'How do we stop him?'

'My darling Fletcher . . .'

'Who *is* it?'

'I don't know . . .' She shook her head sorrowfully. 'I don't *know*.'

Frank tried to calm himself. If he got uptight, there was the possibility of spooking her into silence or hysteria. 'Call him off,' he said gently. 'Stop it now . . .'

'I can't,' she wailed. 'He doesn't even know who hired him. He doesn't know who I am and I don't know who he is.'

Frank Farmer's brow furrowed. 'How'd you do it?'

She was teetering on the edge of hysteria as the enormity of her crime closed over her. Frank couldn't let her sink into incoherence. He stroked her hair and touched her cheek, trying to bring her back from the brink. 'How? How did you do it?'

'I went to a bar in east LA,' said Nicki uncertainly. 'I asked around . . . I talked to a man.'

'Name?'

Nicki was vague. 'A Spanish name . . . Armando. He arranged it. That's all I know.'

'Is it all paid for?'

'And then some . . . Till it's done,' she stammered.

'He keeps going until he kills her?'

Nicki nodded again, then lowered her head into her hands, the picture of misery.

'What was the name of the bar?'

'I'm . . . I'm not sure . . . I was very stoned.'

'How about the letters? How did you arrange those?'

'No, no,' said Nicki desperately, 'you don't understand. The letters came first. I don't know who was sending them . . . but whoever it was was reading my mind . . . His thoughts were *my* thoughts. I hate her. It made me think I could do it. But I could never hurt Fletcher. Never.' She seized his hands, squeezing them tight, imploringly, beseeching him. 'You have got to stop it. Frank, please!'

'We will. You and me. Tomorrow we're going back to LA. We're going to find that bar. We're going to find Armando.' He stood up. 'It will all be over soon.'

'Don't you even want to know why?' she asked.

'You told me. She has everything.'

'What if we can't –?'

'Quiet,' hissed Frank. He was standing still in the center of the room, his gun up. Sparky, upstairs on the landing, was growling.

'Stay here. Don't move.' Silently Frank crept from the room, making for the stairs, climbing them two at a time. Sparky was on his feet, growling, staring in the darkness. Frank threw open the door to Rachel's room, his gun breaking into the darkness.

Rachel sat bolt upright in the bed, clutching Fletcher. There was a sound behind and he wheeled around, ready to shoot.

'It's me!' Herb had his .38 police special in his hand.

'What's happening?' Rachel demanded. Fletcher's eyes were wide with fear.

From downstairs they heard Nicki's voice. 'No, no ... stop! I'm the one who –' Her words were cut short by the roar of gunfire. Rachel screamed.

Henry emerged from his room. 'What's happening? Where's Nicki?'

'Jesus! Herb, stay with Rachel.' Frank dashed for the stairs, pounding down to the ground floor. Nicki lay in a pool of her own blood just inside the open front door. Her blouse was a mass of gore. Frank knelt and felt for a pulse. There was none.

He peered out into the fog swirling in the night beyond the door. 'Dad?' he yelled.

Herb answered quickly. 'We're okay!'

'Stay there.'

Frank darted out into the darkness, his back against the wall of the house. He scurried a few feet and stopped, listening. There, beneath the sound of the wind in the trees, he could hear the noise of footsteps, heavy boots crunching in the snow. He was moving out into the woods. Frank set off at a run, aiming for the sound.

He wove in and out of the fog, running a few feet, then he stopped, waiting long enough to pick up the sound, and then set off again, closing the gap between them. Deep in the woods he stopped again and listened.

Silence.

He froze and raised his gun. Then he closed his eyes and waited, listening so intently he felt he could hear the silence itself.

The instant he heard the slightest sound of movement he fired twice, the big gun bucking in his hands. There was the sound of someone running and the howl of bullets ricocheting off in the darkness. Because his eyes had been closed when he fired, he did not lose his night vision to the muzzle flashes.

Frank could sense the man's fear. He was crashing through the woods now, making no attempt to hide his tracks. Frank fired once again. The engine of a car burst into life, and Frank came running out of the woods on to a dirt track, a fire-break in the forest.

The car was roaring down the trail, its rear wheels spinning in the snow. Frank crouched into the combat stance and fired, again and again, blasting out the rear window of the car, glass flying into the darkness. The shots echoed in the night and the muzzle flashes lit up the sky. The car fish-tailed out of sight, and Frank lowered the gun to his side. His heart was pounding, and he panted, his breath clouding the air around him. The night was cold, yet his shirt was drenched with sweat. But his hand was steady.

CHAPTER TWENTY

Snow fell steadily all the next morning. They had walked out from the lake at first light, and once they had reached the main road Herb flagged down a passing logging truck that had carried them into downtown Bend. The police were already on their way out to the house, and Rachel, Henry and Fletcher were under guard in the station house, drinking coffee, trying to thaw out their chilled bones and trying to forget.

Frank got on the phone to Minella and Court down in Los Angeles. He quickly told the agents what had happened and listened for a moment in stunned silence.

'But, Frank,' said Minella, 'this just doesn't make sense.'

'What do you mean?'

'We already got him.'

'What? Who? Where?'

'Here, last night. He's some loser, works in a car wash. You should see his locker, Frank. This guy is obsessed with Rachel Marron.'

Minella was in an observation room at the FBI center in downtown Los Angeles. He glanced through the one-way mirror at the cell beyond. Dan was sitting at the table in the dingy room. He looked frightened and disoriented.

'You sure it's him?'

'Forensics say it's a 100 per cent positive ID. And he's got a black Toyota 4 × 4.'

'Well,' said Frank, 'whoever you've got down there wasn't here last night. This was professional.'

Frank could almost hear Minella shake his head. 'This is crazy. What do you want to do, Frank?'

'How long can you keep him?'

'Well, technically all he's done is write some letters. Forty-eight hours maximum. You know the deal.'

'Yeah,' said Farmer, 'I know the deal.'

It didn't take long for news of the violent death of Nicki Marron to leak out, and by the time the chartered jet touched down at Los Angeles airport a full contingent of the press was lying in wait for them. Devaney and Spector were on hand to deal with the press, keeping them at bay until Rachel and her party could be whisked away in black limousines.

There were more press and photographers waiting at the gates of the estate, and they shouted questions as the cars passed.

'Rachel, did your sister –?'

'Rachel, was your sister –?'

'Miss Marron, your sister –'

It sickened Frank slightly when he realized that even in violent death Nicki would never be more than sister to a superstar.

At the front door of the mansion Rachel got out of the car, gathered Fletcher and disappeared into Emma's waiting arms. Spector and Devaney vanished into other parts of the house, leaving Frank alone.

He was not a drinker, but he marched through the house and into the family room, the place where he had first been introduced to Nicki, and poured himself a little bit of orange juice and a lot of vodka. He sipped, grimaced and slumped into one of the chairs.

Hours passed, and the sun set, and Frank sat immobile, the ice in his glass melting. A small voice came out of the darkness.

'You okay, Frank?'

Frank acknowledged Fletcher's small presence but didn't look directly at him. He seemed to remember his drink, picked it up and sipped.

'Yeah,' he said finally. 'I'm okay. How 'bout you?'

'Mom told me to go to bed but I couldn't sleep. It was so scary, just thinking about it.'

He looked hard at Frank, staring at him through the gloom. 'Do you feel scared, Frank?'

'Yeah, Fletcher, I do.'

The boy's eyes widened. 'You *do*?'

Frank put his hand on Fletcher's head, as if conferring a blessing on the little boy. 'Everybody is afraid of something, Fletcher. That's how we know we care about something, when we're afraid we'll lose it.'

'What are you afraid of?'

Frank patted him on the head. 'I think you should try to go back to sleep now, pal.'

'Tell me, Frank, please,' the child persisted. 'Is it the man who killed Nicki? Are you afraid of him?'

Frank shook his head. It was not that kind of fear at all – it had never occurred to him. Rather, it was a fear almost unique to him alone.

'What is it?' Fletcher pressed. 'What are you afraid of?'

'I'm afraid . . . of not being there,' he said finally. Then he stood up. 'It's late. Do you want me to take you back to your room?'

Fletcher shook his head. 'No, it's okay.'

'C'mon.' Frank tapped the boy on the shoulder. 'I'll walk you half-way.' Glass in hand, Frank escorted the boy through the darkened rooms on the ground floor to the base of the staircase in the front hall.

As Fletcher started up the steps, Rachel appeared at the top. 'I thought I told you to go to bed,' she said.

'I'm going, Mom.'

As he passed her, she knelt and kissed him, then watched as he walked down the hall. Rachel came down the stairs slowly, her eyes never leaving Frank's face.

Her eyes were red-rimmed with crying, and her cheeks were sunken and gaunt. In that second her nerves snapped, and she lashed out at Farmer, slapping at him hard, hitting him in the face and torso. The first strike knocked the glass from his hand. It flew into a dark corner and shattered.

'You, you, you .. , You brought this pain into my house. *Now* you're here! Where were you then? Why didn't you save her?' Her hand slapped his cheek and it stung, planting a red palm print on his skin.

Frank raised his arms in a half-hearted attempt to ward off the blows. He didn't strike back. He just waited until she had vented her anger and frustration.

'It was your job to protect *me* and *she* died. It was *me* they were after. And you let them kill *her*.' She was gasping for air now, and her blows were becoming sloppy and weak. 'She never did anything to anyone,' Rachel wailed.

As if she couldn't summon up the strength to stay on her feet, Rachel sank down to the floor, sitting on the bottom step of the staircase. 'She never hurt anyone,' she moaned through her tears. 'She never wished anyone any harm. Did she? *Did she?*'

Frank shook his head. 'No,' he said quietly. Rachel would never know what Nicki had planned for her; she would never know that Nicki had brought death into the household.

Frank sat on the step next to her and put his arms around Rachel. She struggled in his embrace for a moment, then gave in, laying her tear-stained face on his shoulder. 'She never hurt a soul . . . I didn't love her well enough. I didn't take care of her . . . She only gave me love . . .' She spoke slowly, weakly, like a clockwork toy winding down.

Finally, she was silent for a long time. Her tears dried and her breathing slowed. Frank was beginning to think that she had given into the emotional ravages of the past hours and had fallen asleep, dozing in his arms. Then she spoke.

'It isn't over yet, is it?'

Frank nodded. 'He knows he still hasn't got you.'

'So he'll come again?'

'It's possible,' Frank acknowledged. There was no point in lying to her, in underestimating the dangers she still faced.

'The Oscars?' she asked.

'Maybe.'

She gave a great, heaving sigh. 'When I was back home – back when I was nobody – I started betting my friends fifty bucks each that someday I would win an Oscar. You can understand how important it is that they see me up there if I win.' Rachel managed a crooked smile. 'If every one of those pikers comes through, it could add up to a lot of money.'

'I think it's very dangerous,' said Frank.

'I know . . . But I can't stay up here on my hill for ever.' She shrugged. 'I didn't get to this place in my life by doing the smart thing every time.'

'I can understand that.'

'You can? You, Frank Farmer? You ever do the same thing, out there on the edge? Did you ever do something that didn't make too much sense, except maybe inside you?'

Frank didn't answer.

'I'll bet you have plenty,' she said filling in the

silence. 'Nobody gets really good at anything without taking chances. And I know you're good.'

'I try.'

'I don't know why all this has happened to me. But I guess I realize that it's not your fault . . .' She smiled again. 'I'm sorry I hit you. I'm . . . It's just that . . .'

He smoothed her hair, a small gesture that told her that he understood, that it was all right.

'So . . . I'm going to go see if I win an Oscar. And I won't worry about it at all. Because I've got you to protect me.'

Frank smiled. 'That's right.' He lowered his face to kiss her and laid her down on the soft rug of the hall, moving his body over hers, like a bodyguard protecting her from the evils of the night.

CHAPTER TWENTY-ONE

It's the biggest night of the year in Hollywood. The Oscars are a long, glitzy, expensive celebration of the entertainment industry, a jubilee party dedicated to self-congratulation.

By the time the broadcast itself got under way, the whole town was caught up in a frenzy of celebrity. Limousines were lined up for six blocks near the Pantages Theater, inching forward to the red carpet that led from the curb into the venerable auditorium. On either side of the runway and facing the theater across the street were tall grandstands packed with fans who had assembled there in the early morning to make sure they got a front-row seat.

The area in front of the theater was packed with police and security men, television crews and reporters. The instant a limousine door opened, a master of ceremonies pounced, looking to see if the car contained a star or a mere director, producer or screen writer. A celebrity set the crowd off. They cheered and chanted and flashbulbs popped like gun fire. Anybody else was greeted with indifference.

All the men in Rachel's limo wore black dinner jackets, faultlessly tied black bow ties knotted at their neck. Rachel Marron – both a nominee and a presenter – was dressed in a spectacularly sequined gown, a breathtaking red-and-silver sheath that left her neck and shoulders bare.

They could see the hubbub at the entrance of the Pantages – TV cameras, lights, photographers.

The glare and the arc lights were almost blinding.

There was tension in the car, but it only seemed to affect the men. Frank noticed that Rachel seemed relaxed yet high-spirited.

'We'll go straight to the Green Room, right, Frank?' The Green Room was the enormous room backstage where the celebrities waited until they were called on stage.

'That's right,' said Frank.

'Got that, Tony?' Devaney turned to the big man. 'Understand?'

'Tony knows what he's doing,' said Frank quietly.

Tony looked surprised and not a little pleased at this unexpected vote of support.

As the limousine crept a little closer to the threshold of the theater, Rachel gave a little laugh. 'I wish you boys would relax a little. Nothing bad is going to happen out there, all right? Understand?' She thought a moment and then grinned. 'Unless I don't win that fucking award . . .'

No one laughed. She looked from one tense face to another. Not even Spector was up to doing his star stroke. 'Jesus,' she giggled. 'What a crew.' She flipped down a vanity mirror built into the side of the car and examined her make-up. 'Screw it. I'm through worrying. When your number is up, it's up. Right, Farmer?'

Not if I can help it, Frank thought. The car had almost reached the carpet and he slipped out of it before it stopped. He stood on the sidewalk and surveyed the scene. There were people everywhere and any one of them could have had a shot at Rachel.

The car doors swept open and Rachel stepped out. 'Miss Rachel Marron!' announced a master of ceremonies.

There was an immediate wave of bright light and

applause. Hands reached out to touch her, autograph books were waved at her.

'Everyone wishes you the best tonight, Rachel,' said the announcer.

'Thank you!' Her smile was convincing, lovely and radiant. Spector, Devaney and Tony fanned out around her looking strained, as if they were attending a funeral. Frank led them into the building and out of the publicity storm. The first test was over.

The Green Room was packed with people milling around the bar and the buffet, waiting for their turn to appear before a billion people. It was the kind of thing that tended to make the most jaded show-business professional a little nervous, so people talked a little louder and faster than they would normally. Some drank too much to calm their nerves; others, fearful of not being in control on television, drank nothing more powerful than mineral water.

Eyes kept on flicking to the most prominent feature in the room – a huge TV monitor that showed the action on-stage and, next to it, a large clock ticking off the seconds.

Skip Thomas, the associate producer of the show, hurried up to Rachel. 'Hello, Rachel. I need to get you straight on your responsibilities.' Thomas wore an earphone-microphone headset and he looked harried and exhausted.

'Sure, Skip.'

He handed her a typewritten sheet and consulted a clipboard as he spoke. There, laid out minute by minute, was the order of the evening's events. Each minute of the show was plotted down to the second.

'Okay,' he said. 'We've got Best Sound, then another song, then you. At precisely 8:07 you'll be presenting with Clive Healy. The prompter will be straight ahead of you and – we pray – working perfectly.'

Rachel nodded and smiled. 'Fine. Got it. You'll be a big shot someday, Skip.' She glanced at the clock. 7:43. 'Hey, Clive!' She waved at the slim British actor.

Healy kissed her hand. 'I understand it is my great honor to escort you on stage.'

'That's right, Clive. And I don't like it one little bit that you look skinnier than me . . .'

Healy laughed. 'The camera adds ten pounds, you know . . .'

'Thanks for reminding me.'

On the monitor, a man and a woman were accepting the Academy Award for sound editing. These people were the non-coms of the film industry, anonymous for most of the year, who got to speak out only once. They were making the most of it, spouting the usual long, rambling, slightly embarrassing acceptance speeches.

'Rachel,' called Skip. 'One more song and you're on.'

'Got it.'

It was time for Frank to do his job. 'I'm going to have a look around,' he told Tony. 'I'll come back to her. Stay alert.'

Tony nodded. Frank walked down the corridor that connected the Green Room with the stage. There were people everywhere, men in tuxedos, techies in blue jeans and running shoes, dancers in exotic costumes waiting to go on stage. Portman was there also.

'What are you doing here?' Frank asked.

'I'm on the job,' said Portman.

'Who?'

'Him.' Portman pointed to a monitor. The host of the show, a world-famous actor named John Reardon was on stage, announcing the next act.

'Short-term gig,' Portman said, watching his employer get some easy laughs out of the audience, 'but quite profitable. Listen, Frank, I'm sorry about Miami. You know, nothing really happened. I felt bad for you. I wanted to say something at the time, but you had disappeared.'

Frank shrugged. 'Water under the bridge.'

John Reardon came offstage, wiping his brow with a silk handkerchief. He glanced at his bodyguard and Portman straightened up, tightened his bow tie and winked at Frank. 'Back to work,' he said. 'Probably see you at the Governor's Ball.'

Farmer watched him go back on and raised his sleeve, speaking into the Surv-Kit. 'Tony? You there?'

Tony's voice came back immediately. 'Yeah, Frank?'

'Tony,' said Frank evenly. 'I've got the feeling this is the night. I think he's gonna go for her in front of all the cameras.'

'No shit? That's crazy!'

'It's the kind of thing only a lunatic would do. That's how he wants it to look. Except he isn't a lunatic. He's very clever. I need you to help me.'

There was not the slightest hint of competition between the two men now. 'I'm with you, Frank.'

A sound technician tapped Frank on the shoulder. 'You can't use that thing back here.' The man was agitated and sweating heavily. 'The breakthrough is killing our radio mikes. You're gonna have to disconnect that.'

'But –'

'There are no buts,' the man said forcefully.

Reluctantly, Frank shut down the Surv-Kit. Now he was on his own, isolated in a sea of people.

CHAPTER TWENTY-TWO

Frank hurried back to the Green Room. One look at his face and Rachel's calm, unruffled composure vanished, as if he had transmitted his anxiety to her. Suddenly, she was frightened, scared of what might happen in the next few minutes, terrified that the next few minutes might be her last.

'What's wrong?' she demanded.

Before Frank could answer, Skip Thomas bustled up. 'Rachel . . . Clive. Let's go, okay?'

Frank and Tony closed protectively around Rachel.

'Really,' said Skip Thomas irritably. 'Must we have everyone? We have our own men on the door. Rachel, isn't *one* bodyguard enough?'

'Tony stays,' said Frank, shortly.

'I want him,' said Rachel quickly. Strength in numbers, she thought. The more protection the better.

Clive Healy took Rachel by the arm. He seemed cool and collected in contrast to her agitation. 'Come, Rachel, let us brighten the firmament . . .'

Rachel forced a smile and followed Frank up the runway to the stage, Tony bringing up the rear.

Healy could feel the tension in her hand. He patted her arm soothingly. 'Try to relax, Rachel. I know you must be very excited.'

Skip glanced at the clock just inside the wings. 8: 05. 'Okay. Careful going out,' he said, 'someone spilled some water out on stage.'

On the stage John Reardon was just wrapping up his introduction. 'And to present the Best Song award we have our debonair friend from England and the lady who has everything – Clive Healy and Rachel Marron!'

The red running lights on all the television lights clicked on and the music welled up. Applause gusted out of the huge audience. Clive and Rachel walked out into the maelstrom of noise and light. Clive was all smiles, Rachel at his side was trying to relax, but it was plain to see that behind her smile she was distracted, frightened.

The applause died away as they reached the podium. Straight ahead of them was the clear plastic of the teleprompter, Rachel and Clive's lines scrolling silently across the screen.

'Well, Rachel,' said Clive, reading from the machine. 'I know you only came tonight to present this award and you'll want to leave as soon as we're done.'

There was laughter from the audience and then they waited for Rachel's canned riposte. Her lines appeared on the screen but she didn't start reading immediately. There was an awful silence. She was looking into the audience, her eyes darting.

Clive covered for her as best he could. 'Over the course of the evening we've heard five smashing songs and the names of the artists who created them . . . And I know that no matter what anyone thinks, you have no personal favorites.'

There was thin laughter from the audience. They were starting to sense that there was something wrong with Rachel. Her eyes still scanned. She could feel *him* out there and she braced, ready for the bullet to come out of the darkness . . .

Healy plowed on. 'The Best Song nominees are: "Clock on the Wall" from *The Dining Room Table* by Dana S. Lee and Sara Spring.' Healy paused for a moment waiting for Rachel to pick up her cue and read the next entry. She remained silent.

'"Give Me Your Trust" from *Out of the Gloom* by David Siegel and Barbara Gordon.' He continued like a trooper. '"I Have Nothing" from *Queen of the Night* by Nancy Gabor. "Maybe Soon" from *Maybe Soon* – Anne Trop and Ben Glass. And "Reflections of My Heart" from *Hot and Cold* by Leslie Moraes.'

There was a moment of silence, then Rachel managed to blurt out one of her lines. 'All right, Clive, let's find out. Let's find out who the winner is.'

Clive Healy grabbed the envelope and tore at it, pulling out the card.

In her mind she could see the note, hear his voice. MARRON BITCH. I HAVE NOTHING. YOU HAVE EVERYTHING. THE TIME TO DIE IS COMING...

'I Have Nothing!'

Rachel gasped and stifled a scream. 'And the winner is, "I Have Nothing" from *Queen of the Night*, music and lyrics by Nancy Gabor . . .'

As the lyricist ran toward the stage, Rachel felt herself losing control. She backed away from the podium and then dashed off stage. In the wings people quickly clustered around her, peering into her face.

'Rachel? Are you okay?'

Over the monitor they could hear Nancy Gabor gushing into the microphone. 'I want to thank Rachel Marron. Without her support, encouragement and determination to help get an unknown song writer heard . . .'

Backstage Rachel looked as if the shock was passing, yet she barely heard one of the dancers behind her say: 'I've always said she was nuts. I always said that . . .'

Clive Healy came off stage and immediately went to her. 'Are you all right, Rachel?'

'She'll be okay.' John Reardon was standing next to her with his arm around her shoulders. 'Stage fright. Get it myself.'

'I'm fine.' She dabbed at her face with a handkerchief, recovering fast. She had passed through fear and into embarrassment as it began to dawn on her just what she had done. 'Christ, what an idiot I am. Jesus! What the hell is the matter with me?'

Frank was at her side now. 'Rachel –'

'Farmer, you have turned me into a raving lunatic,' she snapped.

'John,' said Skip Thomas. 'You're on in thirty seconds . . .'

'I have to go back out,' Reardon told Rachel. 'You sure you're going to be okay?'

'Thank you for your help, John. C'mon, Tony . . .' She marched back toward the Green Room, leaving Frank behind.

Reardon was just about to step on stage.

'Where's Portman?' Frank asked.

'Who?' Reardon was staring at the clock on the wall, watching the second hand sweep toward twelve.

'Portman.'

'Never heard of him.' The music came up and Reardon stepped back into the limelight.

Rachel was seated at a dressing table, repairing her make-up, seething with anger at herself for allowing her nerves to take over and ruin her appearance on stage. Skip Thomas was at her elbow.

'Rachel,' he said, 'I'm sorry, but if you're going to be in your seat for the Best Actress award, you've got to go now.'

She dabbed at her make-up angrily. 'Skip, I'm

moving as fast I can. For Chrissakes, go and twitch somewhere else.'

Spector moved in to calm his star. 'Honey, everything is fine. No one noticed anything. Everybody in this building is ready to jump out of their skin from nerves.'

'Bullshit!' she spat. 'You saw me! Farmer's made me into a raving lunatic.'

'Something's going on you should know about –' Frank broke in.

'You're making her crazy. You're making us all crazy.'

'Rachel,' said Frank earnestly, almost desperately. 'I know who he is. He's here tonight. I think he's –'

'Shut up!' She threw down her powder brush. 'Shut up, you maniac. You never stop. Now you've made an ass of me in front of a billion people. And you won't quit!' She stood up and stalked away.

Frank grabbed Tony by the sleeve. 'Tony. It's Portman. Remember? The guy in Miami.'

Spector leaned in between them. 'Tony, after tonight you're back in charge.'

'What?'

Spector shot a withering glance at Frank. 'This man knows *nothing* about show business.'

'Really?' Tony squared off with Spector for the first time in his life. 'But he's not an asshole,' said Tony. '*You* are an asshole.'

You could feel the tension mounting in the theater as the evening drew to its climax. The Best Actress award was the first of the big final four. Next came Best Actor, Best Director and, ultimately, Best Picture. It was the high point of the biggest night in the Hollywood calendar.

Reardon still looked completely unruffled on stage, immune to the strain in the air and as if he appeared in front of hundreds of millions of people every day of his life.

'Presenting the Best Actress award,' he said, 'we have the man who last year received the top honor an actor can achieve for his performance in *South of Waco*. Ladies and Gentlemen, Tom Winston . . .'

Winston, a boyish-looking but perennially popular actor, sauntered on to the stage, smiling broadly and accepting the applause from the audience as his due. 'Thank you, John, thank you, Academy members.' He paused and looked out into the lights for a moment.

'You know,' he said as if he was having a very casual little conversation, 'it brings back some great memories to be standing here again. Last year I figured something out. While it is a great honor to be nominated, actually *winning* caps the evening very pleasantly.'

There was laughter from the audience, but all five women nominated were thinking the same thing: *Get on with it*.

'And the nominees for best performance by an actress in a leading role are – Constance Simpson for

Hot and Cold.' A camera pushed in on her face, isolating Simpson.

'Ellen Pearson for *Maybe Soon.*' Her picture was added to the scene.

Frank had figured out the route the winner would take. He raced through the backstage area and planted himself just six feet from the steps at the edge of the stage. Tony was at his side.

'Rachel Marron for *Queen of the Night* . . .'

Frank scrutinized the crowd. His eyes locked on a man carrying a hand-held camera mounted on his shoulder. The heavy apparatus obscured his face . . .

'Tony,' he whispered, 'I want you on the other side . . . And check out that cameraman. I don't think he's supposed to be there.'

'Got ya, Frank.' Tony trotted off obediently, heading toward the cameraman.

Tom Winston had finished reading the names of the nominees. There was a moment of silence.

Frank drew his gun.

Winston raised the envelope. 'And the winner is . . .'

Tony tapped the cameraman on the shoulder. 'Hey, you! What the fuck you doing here?'

'. . . Rachel Marron for *Queen of the Night.*'

There was a tempest of applause and shouts, a thundering noise that drowned the attempts of the orchestra to play 'I Have Nothing'. Rachel, looking stunned, stood, then bent to kiss Bill Devaney and Sy Spector. People in the row behind her patted her on the shoulder. Slowly, she started the long walk to the podium.

Under the cover of the noise, Portman whipped around to face Tony. Without hesitation he jabbed two sharp fingernails into his eyes. Tony shrieked in pain and his big hands clutched at his face. The last thing he saw was the long, slim barrel of a silenced pistol taped to the side of the camera.

Portman hit him hard behind the ear, jabbing a nerve in his skull. Fire seemed to erupt behind Tony's wounded eyes, then came blackness as he fell to the floor.

Rachel was striding down the corridor now, drinking in the applause and praise. Frank watched her move toward the stage and he desperately searched the crowd. Where was Tony? Where was Portman?

Then he saw him. The assassin was standing in the aisle, twenty feet from Rachel, his camera raised.

People were on their feet now, a forest of clapping hands, obscuring Rachel from a clear shot. Her head appeared between members of the audience, then vanished again into a thicket of people. Portman couldn't see her. Farmer couldn't see Portman.

She started up the steps on to the stage, vanishing for a moment into a dazzling bank of klieg lights. Portman slipped behind her, into the cloud of brightness. Frank could not see him through the glare and couldn't fire blindly into the audience. As she reached the top of the stairs, she was at her most vulnerable.

There was only one thing he could do. Frank ran on to the stage and leaped through the air at Rachel, twisting his body as he flew at her.

'No!' shouted Rachel, her voice shot through with fury and terror.

Portman fired twice, the gun making no more sound than a discreet cough. But the silencer didn't matter – Portman could have detonated a stick of dynamite in the theater and no one would have heard it.

Frank and the bullets reached Rachel at the same moment. He hit her like a linebacker sacking a quarterback, throwing his weight straight into her, the two of them tumbling to the stage in a tangle of arms and legs. Frank grimaced and he felt the hot streaking pain of the bullets as they slapped into his body.

Pandemonium, a wild, uncontrollable bedlam exploded all over the auditorium. Men rushed the stage from all sides. Guns were drawn. People were shouting. TV cameras whip-panned in all directions. The voice of the director in the control room was plain and panicky.

'Go to commercial! Go to commercial!'

Rachel was struggling out from under her bodyguard, pushing herself back up on to her knees. She saw blood on Frank's shirt and felt it warm and sticky on her hands.

A mob had descended on them. Frank felt angry hands snatching at him, pulling him away from her, but he managed to shove her back down and tried to scan the audience, trying to find Portman, who was still out there.

He heard Rachel shout. 'He's my bodyguard! Get off him! He's okay!'

Portman had failed. He knew that the instant he had fired. There was only one thing he could do now and that was to get out intact. He carried his camera toward the side fire exit, well aware that all of the screaming, stampeding people were transfixed by the scene on the stage. No one was paying any attention to him . . .

Security guards suddenly appeared at the doors, blocking the way out. Smoothly, Portman turned away and started for the wings, hoping that one of the stage doors would be unattended or that he would be able to bluff his way through.

Then he felt a hand on his shoulder. He turned.

Blood was streaming from Tony's eyes, but he had his gun out and he did not look as if he would fall to Portman a second time.

'Frank!' the big man bellowed, his voice cutting through the tumult. 'Frank! Over here!'

Frank struggled to his feet and threw off two of the security guards who were tussling with him. For one second he had a clear view of Portman in the open. Frank fired twice.

Both slugs hit home. The first slammed into Portman's heart, tearing it apart. The second struck his head. A shard of his skull glanced off the camera still resting on his shoulder, pieces of which were spiraling out into the audience.

Portman dropped heavily, a spray of blood gushing from his chest, the carpet around him sodden with his gore. The nose of Frank's gun followed him down, ready to fire again. His eyes locked on the corpse, as if unwilling to look away.

Then Rachel threw her arms around Frank and hugged him, the warmth of her tears mixing with his blood.

'You did it,' she said. 'You did it for me . . .'

Frank's face was weary and gray with pain. He lowered his gun, closed his tired eyes and allowed his head to fall forward on to his chest. Nothing more could happen. His guard was finally down.

CHAPTER TWENTY-FOUR

The limousine pulled on to the tarmac of the airport and rolled to a halt in front of the turbo-prop aircraft that rested on the hardstand. Loaders were stowing the last of the equipment for Rachel's band in the hold.

The first person out of the car was Ray Court. It seemed that he had gotten his wish: he had left the Secret Service and 'gone private' – thanks to Frank Farmer. Roadies swarmed over the car, getting the luggage out of the trunk and stacking it quickly in the aircraft.

Court opened the door and Rachel, Devaney and Tony stepped out. Tony wore a heavy leather patch over one eye; the other was bloodshot but mending. With his one good eye he scanned the runway and the small airport building. He scowled at the airplane. RACHEL MARRON TOUR '92 was emblazoned on the fuselage. That would have to go. He had learned some things from Farmer. Court would agree.

Then he caught sight of a figure emerging from the little terminal. 'Hey, Frank!'

Frank Farmer was dressed in blue jeans and a worn old work shirt. Tony could just make out the top of the bandage that bound Frank's bullet-bruised ribs.

'How's it going?' he asked. 'How's the eye?'

'Under control,' said Tony. 'But it won't be the same.' He faked a punch at Frank's chin. 'Ya mutt.'

'Tony ...' Bill Devaney tapped his watch. 'Late ...'

'Some things never change.'

Fletcher and Rachel stood a few feet away as if not wanting to intrude. Tony saw them and clapped Frank on the back. 'Gotta go.'

Fletcher beamed at Frank and Rachel smiled shyly. 'You shouldn't be here.'

Frank laughed. 'Security at the airport wasn't that great.'

Rachel rolled her eyes. 'Security, always security.' There was an awkward pause. 'So, you're quitting show business . . .'

'Yeah.'

'Too bad. You had talent. What are you going to do?'

'I thought I might hole up with my dad.' He patted his bandaged torso. 'Finish that chess game.'

Rachel nodded approvingly. 'You can get him when Fletcher is not around.'

Frank ruffled the little boy's hair. 'That's the idea.'

Fletcher grinned, but tears began to overflow the edge of Rachel's eyes.

Frank shifted uneasily. 'So, how's the new guy?' He glanced over at Ray Court who watched suspiciously, as if he was afraid that Frank wanted his old job back.

Rachel smiled through her tears. 'He's got white hair, Frank.'

'He's very good.'

'But why did you have to get me an old man?'

Frank smiled. 'I don't trust you.'

'Yeah . . . Well, give me a kiss and let's get this over with.'

They hugged awkwardly and kissed lightly. ''Bye, Rachel.'

She turned quickly and walked to the plane, climbing the ladder to the passenger compartment. The steps folded back into the plane the instant she was inside. She dropped down into her seat next to Bill Devaney.

'Now that wasn't so bad, was it?'

The engines of the plane revved higher and the nosewheel began to move. Rachel glanced out the window and saw Frank still standing on the tarmac, watching the small aircraft move away, carrying her out of his life.

Rachel leaned back and closed her eyes. Then she sat up and dug in her purse. 'Wait,' she said.

The flight attendant couldn't unfold the ladder fast enough for Rachel. She jumped the six feet to the concrete, staggering slightly as she hit, the jet's wash whipping at her clothes and her hair. Hardly pausing, she ran back to Frank, throwing herself in his arms. They kissed passionately, her lips hot on his mouth, neither of them caring that there was a face in every window of the aircraft.

Finally, slowly, Rachel drew back. Her eyes were filled with tears.

'Remember when you said you'd risk your life for me?'

'Rachel –'

'I didn't really believe it then. Nobody means what they say. But you did, Frank. You did it. You laid your life on the line for me.'

Frank tried to speak, but she put a finger to his lips, softly silencing him. 'Don't wreck this for me. I don't want to hear any bullshit about you just doing your job. You did more than save my life, Frank. You showed me a way to be. And I love you for it.' She studied his face a moment, as if just by looking at him she could figure him out, understand what drove him.

Then she smiled, aware that she would never really

know. 'There. I said it.' She spoke so softly that her words were almost lost in the roar of the aircraft engines. 'I'll never forget what it felt like to be under your eye. Never.'

Frank smiled. 'I won't be forgetting you either.'

She pressed something into his hand. 'Here . . . I want you to keep this. If you ever need me, you just put this on and no matter where you are I will find you. I promise.'

He looked into his hand. The little enamel cross glinted in the sun. She kissed him on the cheek and returned to the plane.

A few seconds later the engines accelerated, and Frank watched the craft taxi out to the deserted runway. In his ears the howl of the engines sounded like the roar of applause . . .

The last night of the Rachel Marron Tour '92 was three months later, a sold-out show at the Cow Palace in Kansas City. It had been an exhausting time for her and her staff, but now it was over, entering its final minutes.

Rachel stood on stage alone, ready for her final number. In the wings she could see Tony and Fletcher, Bill Devaney and Ray Court. She had come to terms with her bodyguard early on, understanding that the man had a job to do.

But Frank was still on her mind.

'Now I want to sing you an old song . . .' She paced the stage. 'You know, it used to make me feel sad . . . But it doesn't anymore . . .'

The audience was still, breathlessly waiting for the lyrics. 'Now this song just reminds me of someone very special,' she said. 'This is for him . . .'

Then, hushed and husky, slow and sweet, she began to sing 'What Becomes of the Broken-hearted'.

*

A month after returning to Bend, Oregon, Frank Farmer admitted defeat and allowed his father to checkmate him on the chessboard. Herb cackled a little bit about finally beating his son and then asked, seriously: 'Now what you gonna do?'

Frank didn't even think about it. 'I'm going back to work,' he said.

'Good,' said Herb. 'Otherwise your feet will go to sleep.'

You have to work your way back into the Presidential detail of the Secret Service, like a baseball player working his way out of the minor leagues. Frank's first assignment was on the rubber-chicken circuit, protecting a Congressman from Iowa who had annoyed some of the more prominent members of a Midwestern organized crime syndicate.

Galen Windsor had agreed to speak at a Rotary Club dinner at the Crescent Hotel in Iowa City despite the fact that he had received death threats.

Before he spoke, a local priest delivered the invocation, a blessing on those upright farm-belt businessmen and their courageous Congressman.

'Heavenly Father, please bless us this night as we meet in friendship and duty. Whatever dangerous endeavors those among us undertake, let them never be without your sanctuary. For we all know in our hearts that even though we may walk through the valley of the shadow of death, you are with us . . .'

Frank Farmer, standing behind the Congressman, stared out into the audience, looking from face to face, alert and vigilant.

'We know that you are guiding and protecting us . . . Amen.'

'Amen,' said Frank Farmer.